CW00566387

Balancing on the Edge of the World

Elizabeth Baines

SALT

CAMBRIDGE

PUBLISHED BY SALT PUBLISHING
PO Box 937, Great Wilbraham, Cambridge CB21 5JX United Kingdom

All rights reserved
© Elizabeth Baines, 2007

The right of Elizabeth Baines to be identified as the
author of this work has been asserted by him in accordance
with Section 77 of the Copyright, Designs and Patents Act 1988.

This book is in copyright. Subject to statutory exception
and to provisions of relevant collective licensing agreements,
no reproduction of any part may take place without the written
permission of Salt Publishing.

Salt Publishing 2007

Printed and bound in the United Kingdom by Biddles Ltd, King's Lynn, Norfolk
Typeset in Swift 9.5 / 13

*This book is sold subject to the conditions that it shall not,
by way of trade or otherwise, be lent, re-sold, hired out,
or otherwise circulated without the publisher's prior consent
in any form of binding or cover other than that in which
it is published and without a similar condition including this
condition being imposed on the subsequent purchaser.*

ISBN 978 1 84471 394 3 paperback

Salt Publishing Ltd gratefully acknowledges
the financial assistance of Arts Council England

1 3 5 7 9 8 6 4 2

For John

Contents

Condensed Metaphysics

We're all drunk and Ellie's drunkest. She runs up to a guy with a begging cup outside the Babylon and asks him to lend us some money, we're hungry and want a pizza and none of us has got any cash.

He's about her own age, nineteen. He shakes his head matter-of-factly in his tight woolly hat. He doesn't find her request unreasonable. He holds out his styrofoam cup to show us only a few coins.

Ellie gets talking. He says he's been there an hour. Ellie is shocked that this is all he's got on a busy road in an hour, albeit at night. She's disgusted at this evidence of the bad side of human nature.

He puts his hand out to console her, like somebody's father. He says, 'Nah, you can't blame people. Let's face it, it's a question of empathy, and if there's one thing people aren't trained for in our society it's empathy. They just don't see the relevance of me to themselves.' He shrugs, settling his shoulders inside his army greatcoat. 'And then, if they ever make a start on having a bit of empathy, well the next stumbling block is fear. They see me, they catch a glimpse of what can happen to a person, and they just don't want to know. They shut it off. They look through me, they prefer to make a wide circle round me into the gutter and risk getting run down.'

Ellie nods. The rest of us stand around, listening and waiting.

Ellie says, 'Yeah, and those who do give only do it to make themselves feel good.'

'Oh well,' he says, 'you can't go being picky about people's motives. Selfishness is a basic human survival technique, after all. If someone's semi-selfish action is going to get me through the night, I'm not going to go and question it.'

'Where do you spend the night?' Ellie asks.

'In an alley up Chinatown. It's OK. Take no notice of all that stuff your hear about the Triads, it's all propaganda. That's another thing: fear breeds fantasy, and fantasy's what ninety per cent of the human race is living on right now.'

Ellie says we'll get him a pizza, and we leave him outside and go on into the Babylon to buy the pizzas with a card.

Ellie goes up to a guy with lank hair at the central counter ripping into his pizza like there's no tomorrow or even tonight. He looks pleased and agitated all at once by her approach, his mouth moves about in a slipping grin. Ellie strikes up a conversation. He says he's a researcher. She asks him in what, and he seems to say condensed metaphysics.

Ellie cries, 'How d'you condense metaphysics?'

There's an old bloke at the side counter, even drunker than Ellie, his face fossilised purple. He perks up, he joins in, he says eagerly, 'I'd like to know that too.' He swivels on his stool then lurches and rights himself. 'This is a question I've thought about a lot.'

The researcher grins his haphazard grin and carries on as if he's in the eating Olympics. Maybe he wants to get out of here fast.

A thin thirtyish guy in a threadbare jacket comes over from waiting for his pizza at the counter. He says, 'What's metaphysics?'

'Ideas, man!' says the drunk guy, clinging onto the side counter to stop himself slipping again.

The young cooks behind the counter are grinning and flapping the dough about without looking. 'Isn't it morals?' asks one of them.

The other, looks the elder educated brother, smiles indulgently and puts him right. 'It's all about Being.'

'Eh?' One of the drunk's legs slips off the seat again, and the thin guy goes to help him straighten up.

'Being,' says the elder pizza maker, flinging the dough up. 'What it is to exist, and what you can and can't know.'

'Right!' cries the drunk triumphantly. 'Exactly what I was saying. Thing is, you get these big ideas, don't you? I did. About what I was going to be. And what I needed to know to get to be it. I was going to be famous. I had this big idea I was going to go off to college to be a painter. I had it all planned. But then this happens and that happens, sometimes through your own mistakes, sometimes through no fault of your own, you've lost your chance. Next thing you know, someone's telling you: you can't have this, you don't know that, and too bad your old man died and you had to start work at fifteen. That's what happened to me. I went straight down the pit.' He waves his hand, explanatory, drawing us all in. Everyone's listening. 'And then too bad if the government shuts the pits down. Too bad if it drives you to drink and then your old lady runs off with some bastard still in work. Kaput.' He speaks without bitterness, he stretches his arms in amiable illustration.

The thin guy nods with friendly gloom. 'Yeah, and no retraining programmes, either.'

'Blow retraining! You think anyone could ever retrain me?' He sweeps cupped hands down his front, showing himself off to us. His old raincoat, crusted and stained, was once good worsted. 'No, no, mate. This is what I'm saying. What's stopping me now is what I've become. What I *metaphysically* am.'

'So,' he concludes. 'This is what I've always thought: maybe it's better not to let your ideas get too big in the first place. Better to condense them before the bastards condense them for you.'

One of the cooks calls the thin guy for his pizza.

Ellie's so hungry she asks the researcher, 'Can I have some of yours?' He doesn't have a lot left to share. She takes a piece of pineapple, and he looks half-flattered, half-dismayed.

'Here, have some of mine, love,' says the drunk, and he gets up from his seat, surprisingly steady, reeling only once, and comes and stands between them, looking from one to the other, one hand on the shoulder of each.

A piece of green pepper drops from the researcher's pizza and rolls on the floor. The drunk cries, 'Whey!' in sympathy, and gives a dip with his knees to show he'd pick it up if bending down wouldn't finish him off.

The thin guy comes back and seats himself at the central table, spreading his pizza carton carefully. Everyone watches comfortably and waits till he's settled eating.

'You all want pineapple?' calls one of the pizza cooks to our gang.

We can't decide.

'Go on,' advises the drunk.

'What do you think?' we ask the researcher, who's had it. He grins and shrugs, both nods and shakes his head.

Some of us decide on pineapple, others decline.

'So,' the drunk asks the researcher, now that's decided: 'How d'you do it then, condense metaphysics?'

The whole room is intent, listening. The researcher swallows, chokes, coughs. He's finished his pizza now, he's pushed his carton aside. He's suddenly serious, and he's not going after all.

'You misheard me,' he says. 'I said condensed-matter physics.'

'Oh!' shouts everyone. 'Oh!' We all step back, in hilarity. There are mirrors all round the room and our falling figures loom up and away in them, tumbling and silvery. The cooks laugh, still points flinging handfuls of bright vegetables, yellow, green, red.

We converge back on the centre counter.

'So what's condensed matter?' we all want to know. We are thinking of Alice in Wonderland, and that film where a team of scientists in a submarine gets shrunk and journeys through someone's body. We are thinking of total possibilities, of other worlds and outer space where the rules might all be different. The fries sizzle behind the counter; one of the cooks spins pizza dough on his finger ends.

'This,' says the researcher. He picks up a crust he left. He touches the table: 'This. Or this.' He turns up a coke can and lets the brown liquid splosh on the formica. 'Even the air.' He spreads his arms as if to hold it up. 'Solid matter, liquid and gas.'

We are disappointed. 'Oh, you mean everything. Ordinary, everyday things.'

The purple-faced guy draws his finger through the coke puddle in a contemplative, deflated way.

'No, no, not *ordinary*!' The researcher's eyes are bright beads now. 'That's just it. It's not *ordinary* at all! We know *practically nothing about it*! It's where science has gone wrong! Particle physics is the physics of reductionism! All the time and money poured into isolating particles and working on the crazy assumption that if you know about a single particle you know about the whole! As if in any practical world beyond the particle accelerator particles ever exist in isolation! I mean, you tell me, is that a clear case of bollocks or not?'

The drunk concedes cheerfully: 'Not many bollocks exist in isolation.' Then he changes his mind: 'Tell a lie. We're all castrated in this society. Pardon me,' he adds to us women: 'metaphorically speaking, that is.'

The researcher grabs his arm. 'No, no. Even if you chopped 'em off, your bollocks wouldn't exist in isolation. To put it crudely, I mean crudely in terms of physics: they'd be affected by wherever you put them, and vice-versa: think of the molecules of air they'd displace when you whipped 'em away.'

The thin man winces, and even Ellie draws a breath.

The researcher's voice lowers. 'It's an area of science that's hardly begun to be studied. What happens in solid condensed matter to the *relation between the particles* when outer forces are brought to bear on it? Do they spiral, what kind of changes occur in their lattice work? And how far from the source does the chain reaction stop? You simply can't find out about relationships by studying components in isolation.'

We all sit thinking about it.

Our pizzas are ready, suddenly.

We grab them, share them out.

'Where's the one for the guy outside?' asks Ellie, looking round.

We haven't ordered it.

Ellie's full of remorse. It was her idea and she went and forgot. She asks us each to save him a piece.

'Sod that,' says Anne. She's been very quiet up to now. She takes her pizza off to the end of the counter in the corner. She looks back, challenging our stares. She says, 'Look. I'm unemployed, I'm a single parent, I'm living off benefits, though I'd hardly call it living. On Saturdays I clean up other people's dirt to pay for my kid's school shoes. I don't get treats like this often, this pizza's a treat I can't really afford. Let me tell you, however bad I might feel about not sharing it with a beggar, doing so would make me feel a whole lot worse.'

Now everyone's subdued. The researcher looks around uncertainly, and then gets up. A piece of sweetcorn stuck in his lapel drops off. He goes without so much as a see-ya. The cooks have their backs turned, indifferent cooks now for anonymous crowds.

We eat up in silence.

All except Anne, we each keep a piece of pizza, and gather them together.

When we get outside, the guy with the cup has gone: the spot where he stood is vibrating with blankness, and Oxford Road's a dark vacuum, sweeping towards Chinatown.

The Shooting Script

Sometimes I think I see Bob Deal, glimpse him in a bar or just before he turns a corner, but it can't be, can it? He'll have a whole new life by now, a new name I bet, in a different city where no one's on to him yet.

Everyone wants to make a film, don't they? So it wasn't such a daft thing to do, answer that ad in the listings mag: a chance for nobodies (as long as they were women or black or disabled or homosexual) to get into film making, with a leg-up and a stamp of approval from professional bodies and a guarantee of a TV slot if you were chosen.

I was a woman. I was preparing lessons for my part-time low-paid teaching job, after putting the kids to bed and hanging up Sam's PE kit to dry for next day, when the phone call came with the news that I was one of the chosen. Bob Deal congratulated me in that light, reasonable and respectful man's voice I'd got used to from the commune in the house next door, though with an additional warmth and, I don't know, something glamorous . . . *urbanity* . . . and explained that the scheme had been carefully and specifically constructed to counteract cultural disadvantage by taking full account of participants' life obstacles, with timetables drawn up accordingly and in full consultation. Then he said I was required to attend the first scheduled meeting a week today, when he would like me to have a full treatment ready for presentation.

I almost explained that in those six days I would have several life obstacles to writing a treatment—among them three full days at work and Sam's school concert which as a single parent it was my sole bounden duty to attend; but I didn't. Bear with me: it was always possible that there were crossed lines somewhere, and any man who could be hooked (as he said he was) by my idea for a film about a woman who wreaks revenge on men could only be given the benefit of the doubt. Besides, I was flattered; the man clearly thought me capable of it, and it had the smack of Hollywood, didn't it, sitting up all night at the computer and bugger the routines, and having a good excuse to tell the kids to get their own tea.

Bob Deal had an office in a building let out entirely to community-based and grant-aided projects; there were grilles across the windows and once you'd got past the intercom blackish nylon carpets and a smell of damp earth coming off the cream walls. But Bob Deal came sweeping in (rather late, half an hour actually) and transcended the surroundings: short and round but impressive in an ankle-length greatcoat and a trilby raked dramatically, pale-blue eyes beaming contact and meaning from a face fringed with a long moustache and shoulder-length hair. He gripped my hand. 'I'm so *sorry*! I can't tell you how bad I feel . . . I've had a problem . . . my partner actually. . . But there's no excuse, how can *I* expect *you* to make allowance for *me*!'

Well of course I *could* make allowance—if anyone knew the pressures of relationships on creative endeavour it was me! I clutched my treatment, mercifully finished, but over which one of my relationships had caused me quite some problem, the beeping of the spellcheck having woken Janey in the night.

I was surprised to find no other participants present at this inaugural meeting, but in his office Bob Deal swiftly explained that, obviously, the prime purpose—the prime *concern*—of any first meeting would be to draw up individual timetables according to specific life needs.

'But first.' He leaned intently across the desk towards me and tugged me with those meaningful pale-blue eyes. 'There's something I have to ask you.'

He paused, with an air of sympathy tempered by reassuring shrewdness.

I nodded and waited.

'I have to know. As a *woman,* telling a *woman's* story, are you prepared to work on this film with a *man?*'

I opened my mouth to answer.

'Because I understand the problems completely. Let me put my cards on the table. I'm gay. Which of course gives me first-hand knowledge of minority discrimination. But however aware a man is, he *has* to have his blind spots. Though let me assure you, I'm willing to be guided by you, *keen* to be guided by you. When it comes to the script, or the technicalities of a camera in this project, I'll be the tutor; but as for the *issues*, as for your *meanings*, well, *you* must be *mine.*'

I was entranced. I opened my mouth again but he put up his hand.

'Don't answer. I must give you the means to make your judgment. I must tell you exactly who I am, and where I'm coming from, so that you can make an informed decision.'

And then he told me about his background in film and gay activism—Derek Jarman had been a *friend*—and that ('And this is important in where I'm coming from') he had learned all about the tyranny of minority groups. 'I mean, this was the most *painful* period of my *life!*' (He flicked his hair with the back of his hand in a quick gesture of despair.) 'I can tell you, from personal, *bitter,* experience that a gay man need write only *one* honest appraisal of a crap film by another gay-activist group member and, hey presto, he's the Enemy Within! Me! *Me* who had poured my *guts,* all my creativity, into the cause; working for nothing, plodding my way round the TV stations, building up contacts, dressing up the cause in a way the establishment could swallow—though that was my greatest *sin*, of course. The *contacts* I could have got them! I mean, I'm *known* in those TV channels, I'm the godfather of the daughter of a Head of Drama, for goodness' sake.'

He paused, shaking his head slowly, and then sharply to rid himself of bad memories and the past and address the present. 'Which is why I've ended up in these parts. I've *had* it with the metropolis, and I've had it with splinter groups, and I'm offering my talents to a wider constituency.'

My heart was thudding, with gratitude, and sympathy, and above all with panic-stricken memory: I told him how I too had suffered such persecution, been expelled from my Greenham group for having a man drive me to the women's camp at the missile base. I could see we were fellow souls. Of course I wanted to work with him, and how!, and it seemed quite beside the point that since (as it now turned out) Bob Deal was the scheme's sole tutor and assessor as well as its originator, that if I *didn't* feel I could work with a *man* then I may as well leave the scheme right now.

He then told me with charmingly cheeky confidentiality of several scandals involving adultery and rival Executive TV Producers, and his sense of irony and mastery of pace and timing won my artistic confidence entirely and made me laugh.

He suddenly looked at his watch. Our hour was up. 'Hasn't it *rushed* by—even though we *did* lose some time at the start!' (Here he flashed me a look of friendly and ironically rueful apology.) 'And aren't we getting on famously! I can see this is going to be a fruitful artistic collaboration!' He said his partner would be waiting, and the way things were at the moment between them . . . well, he wouldn't bore me. He grimaced, and gave a sigh of long-suffering though affectionate exasperation.

I said that of course I understood.

I said, but what about my schedule, and come to that my contract (which he'd promised to bring for discussion today).

He said, 'Sure!' and sat up as though confronted by a gun. He said, as for the contract, contrary to his expectations it wasn't quite completed, and this was only because he was so anxious to get it right from the participants'—the *artists'*—point of view. He'd send it out to me tomorrow, and I could bring up any points about it next time we met.

I said, but we hadn't got a schedule, we hadn't decided when we'd next meet.

He said, no we hadn't, but he was sure I would agree that this meeting had been best spent getting these really important issues thrashed out between us. We'd plan a schedule next week—same time, same place, when we'd also work together on a character breakdown.

I felt confused. I clutched my treatment (about which up until then I'd forgotten) and which I'd read in a how-to book should already include a character breakdown. I handed it over, laying it on his desk.

He looked down as if I'd stuck a dead cat there.

He said (with a shaming hint of pity), 'Let's crawl, shall we, before we have a go at running?' He said I must have misheard. He reminded me that the scheme was constructed to take us through *all* of the stages.

He took it anyway, though, my treatment for a film about male abuse of female bodies, and handed me a tape of *Caravaggio*, a film about a man obsessed with other men's bodies, and said that once I'd seen it I'd know exactly how to make my film.

I watched the film, I tried (unsuccessfully) to see its connections with my own, and the following week took it back through the wind and rain (on three buses, into town and out the other side again).

Bob Deal didn't turn up. When I inquired at the desk, the desk clerk's face lit up at the sound of Bob Deal's name as at that of a long-lost buddy, and I knew myself included in the general bonhomie. A girl in a very short skirt and clonky big shoes passed through. 'Seen anything of Bob Deal this morning?' the desk clerk asked her, and she lost her snooty bored arts-worker expression and twinkled at me like I was one of the club. 'No, I haven't yet,' she smiled apologetically, and with affection. They made me feel lucky to be the one kept waiting by him. They seemed so touched, so even *excited*, that Bob Deal could almost have been there in person after all.

In the end the desk clerk suggested I ring him at home.

His voice sounded lighter than ever, and very far away. I had a vision of him surfacing, from water. Or bed. He sounded . . . well, I was reluctant to think *offended*. He said, 'I'm *ill*!'

I asked what was wrong, though with a strangely guilty feel-ing that I should have known already.

He said, 'I've got *flu!*' He said in a pained voice: 'I've been *try-ing* to ring you at home—though really I ought to be *asleep*—but you must have left already.' He sounded peeved at my having done so. Then, with a sudden note of accusation: 'Have you *done* your character breakdown?'

I said, 'But I thought we were doing it *together!*' (crawling before I ran).

I *heard* him sigh. I *felt* him take a deep breath and modulate his voice before explaining patiently and kindly (though not without a frosty hint of reprimand) that we would need some-thing to work *on* together, when we did. He said, more frostily still, that I would need to get it done by the following week, same time.

I hardly liked to bring up the subject of the contract, which had never arrived as promised, but I did.

Now he got animated, and at the same time confidential. He said that it *still* wasn't ready; he said some of the artists who had seen it already had insisted on having a couple of points changed; it was nit-picking only, but he was naturally anxious to observe the rights of artists—this was an artist-*centred* scheme. 'Though you *can* go too far! Some of these artists, they're so *precious,* you've no idea!'

So I didn't have the nerve to say that for me the same time next week would mean changing a clinic appointment of Sam's.

I changed the clinic appointment, I worked on my character breakdown.

Next week Bob Deal was there.

He kept me waiting.

He didn't come through to the foyer, when the desk clerk buzzed him he asked him to send me through.

Bob Deal was seated at his desk in a manner that could almost be said to be grave. He greeted me formally.

I handed him my character breakdown. He scanned it in silence.

These were my main characters: a damaged heroine and her two dastardly lovers, one a plain selfish brute and the other a dangerous emotional manipulator on whom she takes revenge in the end.

Bob Deal looked up gravely. He said, 'I don't think you've made the best choice of characters.'

I said, 'Sorry?'

He said, 'You need to drop one of the lovers, the one called Bill. It's uneconomical, it's a repetition.' His eyes softened, powder-blue, to the expression of a kindly doctor with a painful but miracle cure. 'I suggest you make Bill gay.'

I was icy, but I didn't get as far as reminding him of his reassurance regarding *meanings*. He was one step ahead of me. He didn't miss a beat, he jumped up from his seat, he rushed to a cupboard from which he pulled out his trilby and put it on his head. He said, 'The form changes the meaning. Visual representation changes the meaning.' He said, 'Watch this.' And he cocked his hat back and swaggered towards me like a cowboy; halfway there he turned away and then swirled back again, transformed, the hat pulled low over his brow, shoulders hunched and, as far as it was visible, a brooding expression. He whipped the hat off and his brown fringed face was blithe as a clown's. 'See? A different visual twist, a different meaning!' I had to admit he looked like a different man every time.

My mouth was open, and I guess he missed the meaning, that I was on to him. He seemed not to notice the icy temperature of my response. He told me happily that since I was a novice with the visuals, then that was the area on which we'd concentrate (the scheme being constructed to cater for individual gaps in experience) and since lipstick was a main motif in my film I should pin a picture of a lipstick on my corkboard to remind me, and stick another on my fridge, and put one in the bathroom—I had to learn to live and *breathe* this film! Could I draw? I said I could. He said, Well, it didn't matter if I couldn't, we would meet that bridge (ie the storyboard) when we came to it, that was to say in a fortnight, but in the meantime could I write a first draft script by then?

He didn't seem to notice the unfriendly tone of my goodbye, or my steely resolve.

I rang of the alleged funders of the scheme. Yes, of *course* they were funding him! The young female arts officer spoke with warmth, and even a ripple of excitement (they were so *lucky* to be funding him!) followed by a tone of amazement that I should question it—question *him!* Her tone grew swiftly censorious. She could assure me categorically of the professional nature of this scheme, and all of them, Bob Deal (here she flipped into coyness), herself and the representatives of the several professional bodies including the TV channel (here she grew briefly unctuous) were working in close co-operation to ensure its success. No, (tightening up again) she hadn't *seen* the contract, but she *did* know *all* about the hitch with it, and it was a mark of Bob Deal's professionalism that he should make such accommodation in respecting the wishes of participants who'd asked for changes, and yes she could confirm (hostile: why *should* she; how could I doubt it?) that *as long as the participants fulfilled their part of the bargain, and in the allotted time-span,* then a TV broadcast was guaranteed.

I felt like the nobody that I was. Who would ever be surprised if a nobody set impossible tasks failed?

I decided to beat Bob Deal at his own game.

I sent the kids to stay with their father and sat up twenty hours a day (it was half-term, luckily) and hammered away and called Bob Deal's bluff and within a week completed a draft for a two-hour film. Then I mailed it to his home address, making clear that I required him to read it before we next met.

Next meeting Bob Deal swept into the foyer in a long flowing shot-silk purple shirt (it was a hot March day), flicking his hair as he came through the door against the light, and pumped quickly on his little legs up the four nylon steps, calling 'Darling!' and planted a smacking kiss on my cheek.

There were a few other people in the foyer, and though my back was turned I could sense them noticing and thrilling, and Bob turned to them and preened, showing off his shirt, and they grinned and plucked and stroked it, a goofy girl in leggings, a tall New Age-type guy involved in one of the free papers, and of course the desk clerk.

Then Bob swept back and grabbed me and pulled me to him and among them, and said to them, 'Do you like my *escort*, isn't she a *darling*?' and they grinned at me goofily. 'She's a *genius*, I'm telling you!'

He dropped them suddenly, turned his back on them and ignored them, and swept me up in his arms. 'Darling, I'm taking you out to lunch!'

I began to protest: the (so far unspecified) *allotted time*, my life obstacles as a single parent, which meant we had to take every moment we could get. He brushed it aside, he brushed my hair from my face (with a familiarity no heterosexist brute would have dared). He said, 'We've *bags* of time! We're miles ahead! You're a genius! You've cut through all the crap!' He said, 'We're made! This film will make us, you and me both, Darling!' He said (cuffing me over-familiarly), 'Hey anyway, lighten up, you've got to stop hanging onto those life obstacles quite so grimly.' He said with a grin, 'Don't be a pain.' And then he put his hand on various bits of me, my arm, my shoulder, my back, my head, while instructing the desk clerk to call us a taxi.

He held my arm as we went through the door which, in breach of security regulations, he'd left wide open; he ushered me fussily and studiously into the taxi, so elaborately camp that I took the angry revving away of a nearby bronze Escort as an expression of homophobic disgust.

We went to an expensive Italian restaurant. He ordered the most expensive wine. He saw my face: he said, 'Don't worry, the scheme will pay. It'll come off expenses.' I guess my face only changed for the worse. He took my hand. He said, 'Look. This is business. But it's also our reward. We can *afford* it. We could have spent *weeks*—weeks of time in the office which would have had to be paid for, and weeks of *my* time, my skilled tuition—getting to where you've got in just days at home on your own! And I'm telling you now, confidentially, that not much money will be being spent where some of the other artists are concerned. They've no *idea*! They can't complete the simplest task, understand the simplest instruction! Some of them haven't turned in a thing! There are those I've hardly *seen*!' He said it was all very well making provision for the disadvantaged, but the trouble with the disadvantaged was that they just didn't know how to avail themselves of that provision—let's face it, some of them were trained to expect things on a plate. He was a *facilitator*, for god's sake, not a fucking spoonfeeder, and it was downright patronizing to deny that there were wankers in the ranks of the disadvantaged as well as everywhere else. To be honest, he doubted he'd get a single film out of any of the others. I was his only hope. I was head and shoulders. (He poured me another glass of expensive wine.) I could see, couldn't I, why he'd been unable to set up the communal workshops he'd planned on, and which I'd asked him about once or twice. There was just no common ground. And it would be like trying to organize a swarm of bluebottles onto one turd in a midden.

I asked who they were.

He said, 'You don't want to know.'

I said I did.

He said, OK then, with a look as if to say *I'd been warned*. For a start, there was a lesbian who hadn't yet turned in a basic outline; there was a black guy who insisted on making a rap film although *that wasn't what had been agreed*, and they simply couldn't get past that sticking point. There was a disabled woman who claimed that the disabled access in the offices (though pride of place with the disabled-access planners) was inadequate, and insisted on holding the meetings in her house, and when he got there on showing off her cooking prowess, so they never got any work done. These people just weren't *serious*. . .

Believe me, I saw through it.

But (don't laugh) I thought I was the better Machiavelli.

By the time he'd talked about all the other (awful) artists, and we'd drunk another bottle of expensive wine, it was getting on for five. He said, 'Don't go, the night's young,' and we went on a tour of the gay bars.

At first we were sociable, swapping compliments with the bar folks, and comparing hairstyles, but then in what he said was his favourite bar we settled down. He told me about his tough childhood: his brutal father and his self-destructive mother (you see, he could *really* understand where my film was coming from) and the damaging relationships he seemed to be doomed to since. His lip trembled as he lit a fag.

Well, I was a Machiavelli, but I also had a heart, and I sympathized and told him my tale in turn: the cold husband (he slid an arm round my shoulder) and the poisonous possessive lover (he pulled me nearer). I snuggled up and felt protected. I was pretty drunk by now, and through my fug I also had a vague impression of the whole pub watching—a gaunt shaven-headed man at the bar glaring evilly, and a huge transvestite nearby in button earrings, white stilettos and a wide grey knife-pleat nylon skirt (the exact outfit of one of my old teachers) skewed as if to get a better view of me and watching with anticipation or amusement as if for a denouement. I snuggled up to Bob Deal and told him about the hardship, after all the tugs-of-love and passion, of ending up passionless and alone with two kids.

He said, 'You know, you're such a fucking drama queen.'

His voice was malicious. I tried to sit up to see his face; he held me tighter so I couldn't.

He said into my hair, but perfectly audibly and publicly: 'You're so fucking *Marianne Faithfull*.'

He kissed me full on the lips.

Someone snorted, and someone else banged a glass down sharply.

Next thing I knew, he was putting me in a taxi and paying in advance. 'Take care of her,' he told the taximan with what sounded like feeling. He clipped the seatbelt around me solicitously.

He jumped back out. He held the door. He said, 'By the way, I meant to say. Your script needs work. The mother ought to commit suicide at the start.'

I was suddenly wide-awake sober. I said: 'But that would change *everything*!'

He nodded. He grinned gaily. 'Name of the game, Darling!' And he slammed the taxi door shut.

If he thought I was going to crawl away defeated he was going to be disappointed. When I turned up next meeting and the desk clerk buzzed him I *heard* the long silence before he collected himself. When I entered the room I saw the blue-white look of panic before he had a flash of inspiration and rummaged beneath the desk and brought up a plastic bag, and, camp and giggling, showed me his recent purchases of boxed underwear: tight black knitted boxer-shorts, a fish-net jock-strap and some kind of bondage thing with buckles. Which did I like best?

I said in a steely voice that I could honestly never choose, and proceeded to reiterate *the need to respect the meanings,* and to state clearly—as he had so enjoined me—what those *meanings* for me, as a *woman,* were. I announced that in consequence we would work on my draft *as it stood.* I added (if he could lie, then so could I) that I had now joined a professional artists' organization and had been advised to insist on a contract right away, and instructed to hand it to them for their perusal before I signed.

He gulped.

He nodded vigorously. He clasped his hands on the desk. His cheeks were flushed. He said, Absolutely: I was quite right of course, he was on my side in this completely, and there was no excuse. It was simply a matter of his computer having crashed— had he really not explained that?—halfway through making the changes which had been asked for, so that (just for the moment) there was no complete version, neither the original nor the new. Then he suddenly plunged into the desk drawer and brought out a bottle of perfume which he squirted liberally on his neck, flicking his head and his hair from side to side as he did. He stopped, sniffed, looked ecstatic, said: 'Don't you *love* this per-fume?' and held it up, mutely offering me a squirt. I shook my head stonily, but my heart was sinking, and he must have seen it, because he gathered steam, he said: 'This perfume is so *calm-ing*! I mean, I have to tell you that I'm upset. I know you're angry about the contract, and you have every right to be, but I *am* upset by your lack of trust! I'm *asking* you—I mean, we *discussed* this—to understand my blind spots.'

He paused. He shut his eyes. And (yes, I *know*. . .!) I thought for a moment he'd given in.

He opened his eyes. 'My personal problems. You can't imagine. . .' He flicked me a look of animated revelation. 'I've been up all night, you know! I think *you* know what it's like to be on the other end of possessiveness. . . I mean, really, this morning I'm in no fit state.'

I said evenly, 'Shall we begin?'

We began.

We worked through the first short scene where the heroine as a little girl watches her mother pandering to her cheating scheming father. We got to the end of it.

Bob Deal looked suddenly distracted, even agitated. He said, 'Do you mind if—?' and picked up the phone and dialled. He seemed embarrassed and tense as he waited for an answer. He twitched round the receiver suddenly and said with what I *witnessed* as nervous gaiety: 'Trev!' Then he was all tentative and soothing appeasement: 'Listen, Trev, I'll be back about two.'

There was a question at the other end which he clearly decided not to answer, then he told Trev brightly: 'I'm working on a *marvellous* script, with a fantastically *gifted* filmmaker. . .' Pause, then (with quite *genuine* surprised delight at Trev's making the connection) 'Yes, that's right! The one you know about . . .' And for some reason he rolled his eyes at me, cocked his head sideways at the receiver and pointed to it: *Get him.*

I was still trying to work it out, and we were going through the second short scene where the little girl sees her father with a vampish lipsticked Other Woman, when the door burst open behind me, hitting the cupboard with a crack like a gun going off.

There was a shaven-headed man in the doorway, poised and tense as a cowboy with his hands curled, but also stalled in furious despair. High spots of emotion flared on his cheekbones, gaunt cheekbones I'd seen before, through my drunken fug in the gay bar. . .

Bob Deal cried, 'Trev!'

Trev threw a look like molten metal in my direction, and then for a long scary moment he and Bob Deal held each others' gaze. Bob Deal (*honestly*) was flushed and trembling.

Trev growled: 'I thought you were coming home.'

Visibly, Bob Deal *made* himself calm, controlled the tenor of his voice. 'Trev, I told you. We're working.'

He went on kindly, but firmly and unmistakably ticking him off: 'We're on a tight schedule here, and I think you *know* that. We're going through a script.'

He waved his hand over the desk to demonstrate, inadvertently drawing attention to the boxes of underwear still sitting there, with their pictures of fit jocks with bulging packets. The reek of sultry perfume, I realized, still filled the room.

Trev wheeled round and slammed. Bob Deal's hat dived off the cupboard.

Bob Deal collapsed. He put his head in his hands, then wiped them slowly down his face as he raised it. He said, 'Look,' and held out his hands, and yes, they *were* trembling.

He took a shuddering breath. He said, 'Do you mind if we break for coffee? I need to recover.'

And so we went to the canteen, where some worn-looking housewives from the Women's Aid group lit up like footlights when he entered and called him over with lascivious offers to come and sample their cherry tarts and big cream puffs, hooting delightedly when he said he was sorely tempted but more partial to rock buns or something with nuts.

They did him a world of good. He was quite cheered up, and regaled them with the story of how he'd recently shocked everyone by turning up to his sister's wedding in a shift dress and high heels, on the arm of Trev in full nineteenth-century colonel's regalia.

A call was put through to the canteen for him. He took the receiver with a flourish. He froze. He said stiffly: 'I told you *three weeks* ago that I need a shooting script by tomorrow.' His tone was so cold that the housewives went quiet at the stature of the misdemeanour he was clearly dealing with. 'Look, I'm sorry if it's a problem, but *you* have a side to keep in this bargain. We have funders waiting for results, we have a deadline with a TV station. You can't mess about with these things—' he stalled an interruption '—and by next week I want a camera crew booked and actors signed, and if you can't do *that* we'll have to call it a day.' He put the phone down. He said to me with feeling, 'These other *artists*!'

I said, 'What deadline? *I'm* nowhere near a shooting script!'

He didn't seem to hear me. He looked at his watch. He said, 'Is that the *time*?' He said, 'God, I'd better go. You saw how Trev was. . .' And I *honestly* can say he looked seriously worried.

Our two hours was up, and we hadn't covered more than four pages of a one-hundred page first draft, leave alone a shooting script.

Well, if he'd got himself in too deep through trying to scupper me with a jealous lover, tough.

I went to a bookshop and stood at the Film shelf.

I put my hand up for the only copy of *How to Write a Shooting Script.* Another hand, a big pale loose one, went up towards it at the same time. I turned to a lanky guy in dark glasses and a bandanna with his head cocked at the floor in resignation. I said, 'I'm sorry, my case is desperate, I'm on an impossible deadline.'

He said lugubriously, 'So am I.'

I said, 'You're not . . .?'

He looked up slowly, the light of dawning blinking off his shades.

Yes, he was. He was the gay man who just wouldn't pull his finger out.

I, I discovered, was the headstrong wilful woman who kept wasting time all round by going off and doing things by herself, all wrong.

We went for a coffee.

I said we should all join forces, enough of this Divide and Rule.

He said, 'Yeah, man,' but he looked exhausted already, just too damn tired to lift his coffee, leave alone write a shooting script in one evening or embark on an up-the-workers campaign.

Still, he said he thought he could find out who the others were. He hadn't seen the contract either, but he thought he could get hold of someone who had.

A few days later he rang me. He said he'd tracked some of them down. They'd all got grievances. There was a disabled woman up in arms: Bob Deal had insisted (he claimed because of the lack of disabled access) that they met at her house, and she'd had to *cook* for him! See, he was paying rental on the office hourly, so any saving he could make. . . Trouble was, though, most of them had lost interest, they'd found it so impossible they'd left the scheme long ago. Oh, and the contract; he seen the original draft: no wonder people had refused to sign it, there was a clause requiring us pay back money to Bob Deal if we failed to complete the scheme.

I said, 'What *money*?'

He gave a lugubrious cynical gurgle.

I said, '*Christ!*'

He said, 'Drop it, man. You'll get nowhere.' He said that Bob Deal had gone to ground. It seemed he'd given up his office, and the answerphone was constantly on at his house. He said, 'Face it, man. He's just another wanker. And we're nobodies, and no worse off than we were at the start.'

I wasn't having that.

I rang the woman I'd spoken to before. I demanded to know how I could be expected to pay back money I had never received.

There was quite a long silence. Then she said cautiously (I could *feel* her trying to think it through): 'Well, of course you would be expected to pay back money that has been *spent* on you.' There was another silence, a shocked one, as though she couldn't actually believe she'd just said that. She went on, a bit uncertainly, 'There's your tuition. . .'

I said sarcastically, '*What* tuition? The scheme's a shambles.' I said, 'And it isn't *me* that's getting paid. . .'

She was so silent for so long that I put the phone down.

Then I had one of my life obstacles: Sam and Janey got mumps, and for four weeks I thought of nothing but arrangements for sick kids.

One day, out of the blue, Bob Deal rang me.

He said he'd organized a Shoot.

I said, But we hadn't got a shooting script, I said we didn't have actors. He said, 'No, no, it's not like that,' He sounded . . . well, *understanding*, he seemed *sincerely* keen to reassure. He said with an air of respecting my feelings and *perceptible* self-deprecation:

'This is a *teaching* scheme, remember . . . Look, I know it's short notice, but could we meet for the shoot at the Tanners Arms, midday Thursday? . . . No? . . . *Sure!* . . . Well, how about Friday? Are you sure that's convenient?'

He was so reasonable, so straightforward, I began to wonder if it was the gay artist with the bandanna who was the wanker.

Bob Deal was sitting waiting for me, alone, in a corner of the Tanners Arms, patiently alert with his arm across him on the table in front of his drink. He got up quickly and discreetly and kissed me chastely on the cheek. He bought me a drink without any fuss.

He seemed like a really modest, straightforward guy.

He sat down. He said, without melodrama, 'I've had a lot of trouble since I last saw you.' And then he told me gravely that the funders had reneged. My heart dropped like a bucket in a deep shaft of guilt.

He said, with an air of relief at having someone to confide in, 'Well, they've caused problems all along. These bodies, they promise the funding, you start on the scheme, and then the money doesn't come. They were supposed to be paying me a salary—well, that's a *joke* word for it, actually. But I've been having to live off my savings, and finance everything—the equipment, the office rental. That's why I had to give up the office—I couldn't go on.'

I said, hot with shame: 'So they didn't pay *you!*'

He said quickly, somewhat glibly, 'Well they did in the *end*, but I'd lost a lot of interest in the meantime'—(and here it came, the note of self-righteousness)—'which it was only *right* I should pay back to myself.'

He said, 'Really, between these *funders* and these *artists*. . . well, I had no *option* but to report to the funders that not one of these other artists has turned in a thing! So they've stopped the funding—withdrawn all further support for the scheme!'

He leaned across the table towards me gravely 'Which is so *unfair*. Why should *you* suffer? I'm not going to let them. It's lucky I still have a friend or two in high TV places. I'm going to make sure your film gets made.'

He leaned back. He closed his eyes. 'And that's not all. On top of this there's my personal life. I mean it's not just the *violence*'—I *swear* there was sweat on his brow—'its the psychological pressure. . .' He leaned forward. He said intently: 'You see why this film of yours means so much to me.'

Then he said: 'Do you know, I might just jack it all in. I mean, really. Do something simple and practical and primal. Drive a lorry. . . Take one of those juggernauts right across Europe . . . I've had it up to here with arts bodies and the media crowd . . .'

A shaft of light swiped our corner as the pub door opened. He said with joy, 'Here's the camera and the film crew!'

It was Trev, impassive in the pub doorway, his eyes like cyborg metal studs.

'Whoopee!' cried Bob, and danced towards him, beckoning me to follow.

It was no surprise to me that the car in which we screamed away was a bronze Escort, and I was in no doubt that Trev wanted to kill me (and himself and Bob if need be). 'Darling, steady on!' said Bob from the front passenger seat, patting him like a tantruming child. I was in the back with the video camera. We turned a corner, and I left the seat and caught the camera in mid-air as I fell back down.

We squealed to a stop at a place where a viaduct went over a canal. I could see Bob Deal had the murder scene of my film in mind.

Bob said, 'Water.' He said: 'Now I want to show you the multiple possibilities for ways of shooting water. And I want you to find the way that is right for you, for your film. For your *meanings*.'

We filmed the water from above, we got on our bellies and filmed it from there; we filmed the rushing outflow at the lock.

All the while Trev lounged, detached and grinning, if that's what you could call the way he had his teeth bared.

Bob pranced on to the lock gates, and I filmed him prancing. He leaned broodily away with his bum sticking out, and I filmed him brooding. He said I'd be amazed at the difference in effects.

Then he took the camera. He said, 'Now you.' He said I should know, as a filmmaker, the precise nature of the experience at the other side of the lens.

He made me step onto the lock gates.

He said, 'Come on, lounge!'

I was nervous and selfconscious. Behind me, the water hurtled down a ten-foot drop. I leaned my elbows on the gates and, afraid of losing my balance, made a stab at satirically bending a knee.

Through the corner of my eye I saw Trev coming round from behind me to look. He leaned against the wall, appraising me and baring his teeth. On the opposite canal bank Bob Deal took his eye away from the camera, though he kept it running. He called to Trev: 'I'm right, aren't I?'

Trev looked me up and down, grinning. 'Yup.'

They were flanking me. They were on opposite banks but they were totally together in this. Black water swelled in front of me; the waterfall slammed down behind.

Trev said, sweeping me with his eyes that had switched on like lasers: 'That tragic fuck-me-don't-fuck-me expression.'

Bob said maliciously, 'That fag-hag droop.'

Trev pronounced with spiteful relish: 'Marianne Faithfull to a T.'

And then I tumbled to it, to what had been going on all along.

I gave in gracefully.

I even admired them, for teaching me my first lesson in knowing when I was beaten.

We went drinking then, all three together, and Trev stopped being nasty.

We knew where we stood.

I understood perfectly that after that night I would never see Bob Deal again.

Next time I tried his number, as I expected I got the unobtainable tone. Some weeks later I *did* ring the TV station—though only because I'm so hooked on closure to be told by a polite but slightly panic-stricken PA that the scheme had failed, having lost everyone a lot of money, since not one of the participants given the opportunity had been able to come anywhere near to making a film.

Sometimes, though, I think I see Bob Deal. The hair will be shorter, the moustache will have gone, but there'll be that jaunty short-legged way of walking, and that way of holding out the chest, as if ready to resist a big wind at any time. . .

Daniel Smith Disappears Off the Face of the Earth

Daniel Smith sets off home on air-bubble trainers. Fifteen years old, out later than he should be, light years blinking through the sodium, but then you've got to cut loose some time, right?

There's sweet frost on the city air and sharp music in Daniel's soul. He's humming the riff he's just been playing on Tom Dunnington's keyboard, remembering the notation coming up on the screen, sperms of sound with the music of the spheres on their tails. Man, has Tom Dunnington got the equipment, a sound system in every room in his parents' six-bedroom home with jacuzzi—a similar system to that which Dan has been advocating strongly to his own folks (so far without success), and which he himself could construct with a set of speakers and several yards of wire, at a cost to them of little more than a couple of hundred pounds and the incalculable advantage of music in every corner to accompany all activities, and consequent immeasurably increased quality of life.

Dan's parents, well known as old-fashioned hippy types, accuse him of belonging to the materialist generation, as if he and not they determined the point in history when he should live his life and teenage years.

Dan knows he's lucky, though, fetching up here, out of all the times and places in the history of the world, at the end of the twentieth century, in this city, Music City, at a point in Western civilisation when technology is giving middle-class boys like him a spin. Silicone chips on a silicon planet where life evolved out of stones dropping by from the stars, talk about luck.

Dan has touched his parents' grudging soft hearts for the gear to help him make the most of it (*Cool, Dan! Easy, Dan!*). He is wearing: a fleece jacket in the latest colours, forest green and blackberry purple, the kind they chain up in the store and have to unlock to let you try on; trainers, black with grey trim and designed for the pounding force of top-trained muscles; and his double-dyed denims—the gear of the hill walker, the international athlete and the Wild West cowboy combined in the uniform of the city. Synthesis City, vibrating electronically to the sounds and sights of a hundred cultures or more.

Dan makes for the part of the suburb they still call the village. A bus vacuums to a stop just ahead, and Dan's dreadlocks shake.

They came out of the vacuum. Two youths just like him, a bit older, a bit taller, out late on the town, probably later than their mothers wanted. A bit less lucky: they don't have watches, they ask him the time.

He pushes up his sleeve and reads the luminous figures on his waterproof, pressure-resistant watch made for a deep-sea diver, and tell them, *Eleven-ten.*

And then, while his head's down, they've got him, one each arm, and they're hustling him down a cul-de-sac, tree-lined and ill-lit, with houses even bigger than Tom Dunnington's, set well back from the common world behind laurel bushes that would muffle any call for help.

Not that he cries for help. He's too surprised; up till now his main reference point has been that his mother's worst nightmares lack relation to reality.

This is the moment Dan knows that although he's always counted himself lucky, he's also always counted on his right to be lucky. His feet slow at the shock and fright of this realization, rather than through any impulse to resist. Something sharp digs in his back, just left of his spine.

One says: *The knife. Get the knife out.*

The other: *I have. Look.* The point digs at Dan's back in demonstration.

They are urgent, there's an edge of panic in their voices. Dan half-thinks: They're bluffing, they don't really have a knife. But he daren't risk it, he can't fathom them, he's only seen a fleeting glimpse of their faces washed into stereotype by sodium lighting, their cropped heads.

They stop him up against a tree, rough bark at his face. *How old are you?* The question snaps at his neck.

Panic swells the darkness of the space beyond the tree. Will they rape him? Will they leave him with Aids?

He says: *Only fifteen.* He is pleading: how suddenly he slides from denial of his youth to desperation for its refuge, how cravenly his soul is slipping in the dark.

He senses their surprise, punched like a small black hole in the air behind him.

Then: *Don't believe him.*

They grab his dreadlocks. *Don't believe you.*

Dirty liar.

Dirty black liar.

Now he's skidding. All the training of his left-leaning parents explodes and fades like a dying star: he wants to save his sallow skin by claiming its white privilege. He bleats: *White boys can have dreads.*

Once again he senses uncertainty tug the darkness between them.

Then, vicious: *Take your coat off.*

They move the weapon away so he can. He almost whimpers as he pulls the zip, sloughs the coat off and exposes his raw sweatshirt torso.

They swoop the coat up; the weapon comes back, grinding on a vertebra.

Now the shoes.

He cuffs the shoes off, kicks them aside, kicks away his cushioned platform, feels the dull pull of earth on his soles. Cold gravel, the dead matter of the planet, digs through his socks.

Empty your pockets.

A few coins of dull metal clonk on the flags. His house keys clatter flatly between the roots of the tree.

They grab the lot.

Where d'you live? The blade prods. *Come on, address!*

If he had his wits about him he'd say *Here*, the house just beyond the hedge, his parents waiting the length of a smooth lawn away, watching out for him, listening. But down this dark lonely street where no one would find him till morning, he needs to call on the way of life that is particular to him, those messy meals on that cluttered table, that precisely eccentric way of talking and joking and quarrelling, contained in a pile of bricks in that particular street that is his, a pulsing marker on the anonymous grid of the land; if he denies it, he's obliterated himself before they do. He says the street name.

Number?

He hesitates. His wits return: *Seventeen.* A number not his own.

The voice of one: *We'll sack the house!* But then the other: *The bastard's lying.*

They throw down the keys.

On your hands and knees!

He bends, lowers himself, expecting extinction at any moment. Grit bites his knees, the heels of his hands.

Crawl for your keys.

They kick the keys, the keys slide and stop, gleaming, some yards ahead.

Before he moves a foot jabs his shoulder, stopping him. *Sit up and beg. Beg for your fucking keys.*

And Daniel Smith sits up and begs. Knees jammed to earth, palms raised, the attitude of slaves down the centuries, and Daniel Smith, descended into lucklessness, embraces it, willingly in this moment, if it will save his luckless skin. *Please, please*, begs Daniel Smith, *can I have my keys?*

Right, crawl.

And he crawls. And his hand touches the keys, cold immutable metal, which after this, after all, will never again open on a haven of certainty even if he survives.

It's so black beneath the tree he can't see his hand as it closes on the keys. He opens his palm. The keys gleam, they seem to float, unsupported.

He half-sits on one ankle, holding out his own invisible hands.

He becomes aware that the attention of the youths is no longer on him. He dares to turn.

One is wearing Daniel's coat and pulling on Daniel's ninety-pound shoes. There is a moment in which Daniel Smith's scattered soul thuds back together in material outrage, rich-white-boy fury. They sense it, they look up. He sees fear hit them like a freak wave.

And they're off, down the end of the road
    silhouettes
        flicking out on a sulphur circle
            and then they're away, assimilated in a city of
                      flicking images
           and pulsing sounds

and
        Daniel Smith is dissolving
           while prehistory glitters out of the sky.

Power

Today my powers increased.

Next door's cat was picking its way along the fence and I sent it my beams. It stopped. It couldn't move. One paw half-up and its tail stuck in one place in the air.

We were in the garden because Mum was on the phone again. 'Why don't you play outside?' she said, as soon as she'd answered it, so we knew it was Cassie, and she'd be on the phone for half an hour or even an hour, saying the same things over and over, every so often dropping to a whisper—she thinks we can't hear, she thinks we don't know she's talking about Dad. And sighing: the way she makes a flat hiss and it squashes all the air around so your lungs get squashed too.

We stood still in the doorway and didn't go, we didn't want to. She looked irritated and a bit upset. Then she said, 'Go on, there's good little girls,' in a pleady question not an order. And somehow then my chest felt lighter, and that was when I guessed my powers had grown.

'OK,' I said, and we whipped around and went.

As we stepped outside, the cat leapt up the fence towards us in a swoop of orange as though he just couldn't help it, and came face to face with us, and almost toppled on the edge, his yellow eyes wide with shock.

He tried to resist. He turned away, stuck his tail in the air and showed us his pink bum-hole and started tip-toeing towards the shed roof.

And then I did it, and he stopped short, right where he was. I let him go again. He turned and stared at me, astonished. He waited, to see if I was going to do it again. He turned away carefully, trying it out. I let him, for now.

After that we went off over the road to the building site where they've uncovered an old rubbish-tip and where we're not supposed to go. It's all forlorn there when the workmen have gone home and you go looking for bits of glass and blue-and-white crockery. If you lie on your belly the diggers rear up like great dragons and the white sky tips towards you in a scary way.

She never suspected. When we got back she was still on the phone, still on about Dad.

We haven't seen him for weeks.

She goes on and on:

> —Well, you know what he's like, Cass. He's hooked on that job. And can you blame him—he's so good at it. He's made that firm millions with the Dine-Air account. All the clients are fighting to have him on their campaigns. And I'd be a damn fool if I didn't accept that it puts temptation in his way. Artists, actresses and models—they all think he's God's gift. Oh no, I've long got used to that. He's always been quite open, and none of them have ever meant a thing.
>
> But this one, this time: for God's sake, he says it's a passion! A continuity girl, for heaven's sake. Now if it were one of the copywriters or a creative designer. But he says he's in love! It makes you want to puke. Well, it has to be something else. Something to do with him. Yes, I know what you think, Cass: mid-life crisis. But I think it's a bit more complicated than that. There's a whole load of unresolved stuff, you know, to do with the kids. He's besotted with those kids. Yet it clashes with all his dearly-held principles of freedom and hanging loose. The kids have opened up an area he simply hadn't accounted for. I think that's the reason he's keeping away. He knows if he comes back once it will break his resolve.

She's suddenly silent. Then:

—*Are you listening on that extension, Emma? Put it down!*

She's on the phone again while we're watching Beauty and the Beast in my room. I don't need to pick up the extension any more. My powers have developed so much I can tell what they're saying through the ceilings and the carpets, and from the rays coming off the telly.

She comes in and gives us a kiss each on top of our heads, just as Beauty is about to do the same to the Beast, and says in a sad-sickly way, 'Have you been in here all along, there's my sweet little girls!' That tight feeling comes in my chest again, and I slip out from under, and say, 'Aw, Mum! It's the good bit, you're spoiling it!'

She says, 'Would you like some chocolate ice-cream as a special treat before bed?'

I feel sort of better and jump off the bed and yell, 'Yeah!'

Though I feel funny, too. Like there's electricity inside me and all the wires about to fuse. I eat so much ice-cream I feel sick.

When Anne's having her bath I go outside and climb up on the shed roof and sit down beside the cat. He looks up and goes stiff.

'Relax,' I whisper, and put my hand on his back. I feel his muscles go soft.

The sick feeling slowly fades.

The cat settles in, but he keeps his eyes wide open, waiting to see what it is I want him for.

It's just starting to stay light at bed-time. The blossom above the shed is coming into bud. Over the house there's a white slice moon. I watch it change from flat white to luminous yellow. I can feel my power settling and gathering.

I keep stroking. The power flows from my hand into the cat, making his muscles ripple-twitch.

His eyes turn green.

I open our back door and lead him inside. His feet make soft puffs on the stairs, like faraway fireworks. I let him into my room. He sits quietly as I close my eyes and work a spell.

He says it's over between them, Cass. Oh no, you can tell from his voice that it's the truth. He's utterly wretched. Well, he knows he's been stupid.

Actually no, we've not seen him—he rang from the States. The Philadelphia office wanted him on their Haven Muesli account. It looks like they might want him over there for good.

Well, that's clearly what finished that squalid little affair. It wasn't the kind of thing it would take much to finish—based on a pathetic fantasy as it was. I guess he grabbed the chance to escape. Reading between the lines, she'd started putting on just the kind of emotional pressure he's always tried to avoid. I think he might have learnt his lesson. I think he might be coming to terms at long last with his own emotional needs. He says he can't wait to see the kids.

The cat curls half-hidden by the heavy white blossom as Dad drives up in his hired car. Dad gets out, we run at him wham. He says, 'Hey, steady on!' He lets us lean on him and make him stumble as he goes towards Mum. She's smiling. He puts out his hand and pulls her to him. They put their arms around each other. In the corner of my eye there's an orange flame shooting, and for a moment I think it's my own excitement, leaping out of me, and then I see it's the cat, running along the boundary fence.

Dad gives us: videos, animal pyjama cases—mine a Colorado bear and Anne's a racoon; a map of Philadelphia to share. Mum smiles and smiles.

He stays three days. On the last day, as he's leaving, Mum says to him: 'Aren't you proud of your girls?' He nods and goes serious and gives us kisses. And then he gets in the car and drives off to Heathrow.

After he's gone Mum comes into my room and says, 'Now what would my wonderful girls like for supper as an extra, extra special treat before bed?'

I don't know why but I scowl and say, 'Oh no, not bed, we wanted to play Beetle!' and my voice comes out whiney, and Anne joins in. Mum looks sort of fed up and panicky.

Then she wrinkles up her nose and asks: 'What on earth's the smell like cat-piss in this room?'

*It just doesn't make sense, Cassie. After it was all so perfect, the whole
weekend! I mean, he agreed, that we had to sort it out, that it was ridicu-
lous messing around like this, and the sooner we go out and join him the
better, now that he's accepted the post in the States.*

*I left a message on the ansaphone, the kids sent him a card. Nothing.
And now this. He says there's something stopping him. Some kind of
block. Well, you know what it is, don't you? It's this whole macho thing.
I'd say he was ill. It's a pathology, he's a victim of a social pathology.
It's not that he doesn't feel, it's that he feels all too strongly. I mean, all
weekend he was bowled over by those kids. And he can't deal with it. A
little bit of distance, and he just cuts off again.*

I need something to focus the power.

I creep downstairs. Mum's fallen asleep in front of the telly,
the college papers she's been marking all around her on the
floor. I open the back door. The moon's high and round and cov-
ering everything with light like spilt milk.

I don't need to call, I can do it with my mind, and the cat
hears with his. He comes. He follows me round the side of the
house, sometimes stopping off to watch for mice, then pour-
ing past me and going on ahead. He knows where we're going.

At the rubbish-tip site he sits at the edge while I crunch
across the ground. Moonlight nips along the broken glass as I
go. I start looking. The cat blinks and waits, flicking his tail. It
isn't long before something turns up, the base of a bottle like a
bright seeing eye. I dig it out and hold it high. It ripples with
moonlight and black fortune-telling shapes.

I look across at the cat. He is watching. He has grown to twice
his size.

I place the bottle on my window-sill, right in the middle.

The blossom turns to hard pips of green. Mum takes us to the
seaside for the day. As we turn out onto the motorway she sighs.
There's a feeling inside the car that makes you hardly able to
breathe. Anne is scowling, and suddenly gives me a nasty kick.
I kick her back. She screams and punches me. I scream as well.
Mum says, 'Stop screaming when I'm driving!' We go on screaming and then Mum says: 'If you don't stop screaming you won't
get any crisps!' We scream about that. She cries, 'Stop screaming
and you'll get them!' We stop. Anne grins and I grin back, but

when Mum throws the crisps to us over her shoulder, they fall on the seat with flat depressing smacks.

At the prom she parks the car. She doesn't move to get out, but sits staring at the sea. We know from this that whatever we ask for now we'll get without even needing to whine or moan. I say, 'Can we go on the donkeys?' and sure enough, in a dull voice she says yes.

Though it's not nice on the donkeys, after all. They waddle and the hairs are rough and rub and hurt your legs and a tired feeling comes up to you through their skin. When we get down Anne goes clingy and grabs hold of Mum's jacket. 'Get off!' says Mum, 'you know how I hate it!' Anne starts crying and clings on harder, swinging out and pulling Mum's jacket wide. Mum gives her a little shove and Anne falls in a deliberate heap on the floor, and Mum has to buy us ice-cream to calm us down.

As we're eating it, Mum says grimly: 'Make the most of it, I might not be able to afford it soon.'

I know what you think, Cass, I know it's unfair of him, leaving me in this state of emotional and financial insecurity. Not knowing what the hell's going on. But I honestly don't think he knows himself. Yes, I know you think I should get myself legal protection, but for a start I don't want to tip him into any wrong decision. And more to the point: I'm not falling into that old trap of making his decisions for him. Helping him hide from his fear of commitment. No, he's got to do it on his own.

Today she sells the car. Now she's got to go to college on the bus, and the next-door neighbour will be taking me and Anne to and from school. I watch from my bedroom window as the man who buys it drives it away. Its movement ripples like vicious snakes in the glass of my bottle.

But there's an orange ripple, too: the cat's tail, reflected, flicking as he sits on my bed.

Even Mum notices what's happened. She comes into my room and sees him and cries, 'Ugh!' He jumps up and darts out, past her, and she shrinks back and shrieks, 'What's that monster doing in here?'

He has grown even bigger. His fangs are longer.

The telephone rings. It's not Cassie, it's Dad. And this time Mum's surprised and excited. She says: 'What? This weekend? What time? You'll be there to meet the kids out of school?'

We come running out of school. They're waiting, together, in the hired car. They're both smiling. I say quickly to Anne: 'Don't ask for an ice-cream,' and she says, just as quickly, 'I wasn't going to.'

We run up, and we can see through the glass that although Dad's trying to be jolly, his grin is like a slit punched in cling-film.

I can feel before she does it that Anne is going to ask for an ice-cream after all, even before we've kissed Dad hello. Mum looks shocked and says in a quick bright panicky voice: 'Of course, my darling, of course!'

Dad looks away, and I have to nudge him for a kiss.

But he said it was over between them, Cass! Can you believe it? No hint of it before he got here. And then he announces he's taking her with him back to the States!

No it was over, Cass, I'm sure of it, I honestly don't think he had this planned. It's the same old story: he gets over here, he's sucked in by his feelings, he can't cope, he has to put up a barrier. And of course Madam's still waiting in the wings.

And you should hear it, the rationalization: what he's accusing me of. He dragged up all that stuff about me pressuring him with my maternal desires, I mean, as if it doesn't take two to make a kid. And we had all the usual about me using the kids to tie him down! He says I use them as a weapon, he says it's turned them into monsters. He says, didn't I realise it would drive him away?

We are listening in the kitchen. Greasy pots are stacked every-where. Cold light wriggles in the puddles on the table.

She puts the phone down and comes through, and seems surprised to find us there.

Anne says instantly, 'I want a lolly from the freezer.'

Mum's eyes are wet, but surprisingly she gets annoyed. She says, 'No.'

Anne stamps her foot.

Mum looks fierce and says in a firm voice we're not used to: 'No!'

Anne's so shocked her mouth falls open and her eyes are like two black dots with surprise. All at once there's a new light feeling in my tummy, making me feel I might rise up off the floor.

Anne recovers. 'Aw, Mum!' she roars.

'No!'

The feeling in my stomach pulls itself together in a tight, neat knot.

Anne knocks her mug off the table and spills her juice on the floor, howling like a dog that someone's kicked.

'Pick it up!' I find myself commanding, as the feeling tightens my legs.

Anne screams.

'Pick it up!' says Mum, though she's starting to yell.

And then she goes all limp and weary, and spoils it all by saying: 'You can only have a lolly if you pick the damn thing up!'

Anne stops crying like a switch pressed and bends to get it and gives me a sly quick grin.

I pull back the curtains and let night into the room. Across the road they've built the foundations. All the treasures we might have saved are buried now for good. I turn to the cat sitting on my bed. He looks up with wide eyes. For a moment I think he's frightened, and I put my hand out to stroke him. He backs. The metal-green sparks in his eyes are scary. His fur stands out on end. He hisses and shows his fangs.

Holding Hands

She didn't believe in God.

There were a lot of things she didn't believe in. She didn't believe in holding big sister's hand. 'Get off!' she said irritably, stomping ahead of me, the little wisps flying out all round her plaits. She turned back with a brief fierce scowl, and, though it didn't strike me then, that was probably the moment she made a vow to resist me in everything and do the opposite whatever.

Me, I believed in plenty of things. Then, at twelve years old: God, Romantic Love; I still believed in magic, even though it was six years since I sat with Dad in the car outside the isolation hospital in the hills where they'd taken her with scarlet fever, waiting for Mum to get them to hold her up at the frosted glass for me to see her, and said, 'Daddy, fairies don't exist, do they? Or Father Christmas, either?' He was so surprised and disappointed he missed them holding her up, though all you could see was a naked-looking pink thing, and by the time I'd said 'Look!' they'd whipped her away again. He drove home in a tetchy mood because by stopping believing I'd spoiled all the fun.

Not so. I'd just started to see magic in other things. 'Lin-da!' I called, as she stalked off on long brown legs in white socks and sandals punched with flower holes. I was only mildly hurt, I believed she'd come round, and I was too full of the coming hour, the choir-sound seeping down the stained-glass windows, and my Whitsun dress, gleaming white with red carnations like spots of throbbing desire.

Later on I believed in D H Lawrence, and boys with specs who were sitting Cambridge Entrance and walked me home for Dad's curfew expounding the Big Bang theory of the universe, and who would flinch when we turned the corner and there was Linda with a gang of leatherbacks on parked motorbikes and no intention of obeying what she called Old Gradgrind's orders. We'd have to walk round their legs splayed to balance the machines, Linda's bony in black stockings with an insolent ladder. The lamplight glistened through her beehive as she turned her head to watch us pass. At that moment the leather boys would fall silent, and it was always the moment that Linda would happen to laugh.

This was round about the time she changed her name to Lynne.

Later still, I believed in other things: academia, which she thought snobby; the Common Good, which she found bloody patronizing and even fascist; and finally feminism, which she thought sour grapes, not to mention sentimental. Well, that's what I thought she thought, though she didn't say much when I saw her, which wasn't often, it was a long way, first to Kent, where she went to be a housemother in a school for what she called the bastard arrogant brats of gentry, and then—when she'd run back home—to the college she ended up in after all, being taught to be a teacher by what she called a cupboard-full of mothballed stuffed shirts. And then later when she married a welder, she was always somehow too busy getting his tea.

She didn't say much when I dressed her up in Edwardian leg-of-mutton sleeves to be my bridesmaid, though she definitely scowled when we stepped inside the dark church again, and when she got married she didn't ask me to be hers.

For a lot of years she didn't say much. Not till Dad died.

She couldn't take it. Well, as she said, she didn't believe in God or an afterlife or anything. She couldn't stay with me and Mum and our brother, to watch Dad turning into nothing, his finger-ends going blue and his breath getting ever hoarser and more laboured, and his mouth no longer screwed in contempt or grinning wickedly, but hanging open. She couldn't bear it, she went home. At two in the morning when he finally died I had to call her, and then she said less than ever, there was a long silence while she choked and was unable to get any words out at all.

Well, by then I didn't believe in God either; in fact when you think of all the years that had passed, I'd believed in God for hardly any less time than Lynne; and it was me, and definitely not Lynne, who, in spite of everything, had never quite been able to stop believing in family loyalty, so I couldn't work out what was going on.

When we went next day, she and I, to register the death, she kept quiet; it was me who answered: time of death, who was present or in attendance. Well, it would be me in attendance, wouldn't it, big sister travelled a hundred miles—my kids old enough to be left now—to hold everybody's hand?

Then the newspaper office to collect the form for the obituary, down the back street with the hump-back bridge we used to speed up on our bikes, leaving the ground as we hit the brow. One time Lynne's brakes jammed; they'd never been right since Dad brought the bike from the junk shop because she'd pestered, saying sourly that it was a pity she wasn't old enough or bright enough to get a Saturday job and buy herself one, like me. And then he slitted his eyes at her suspiciously and added: or perhaps he should have said stupid enough. And then the brakes jammed on the hill and she went over the handlebars and bruised her groin, which years later she thought of when they told her she couldn't have kids.

We came out of the news office into the five o'clock December dark. I realized suddenly she wasn't following. I turned. She was hunched in the square of acrid light. I put out my hand. I said, 'Come on.'

She straightened. She said, 'I need a gin.'

So we went to a pub where on Friday nights they used to have a folk club, and for a short time, when the swotty boys had gone to university, and for some reason known only to herself she'd given up the leatherbacks, we used to go there, underage drinking and picking up the musicians—one thing we did do together, because we couldn't do it alone. Though we quarrelled a lot about it, because I thought she was taking unfair advantage, flashing those sexy legs and batting her big green eyes.

Now, instead of cream paint and sawdust, there was a brewery's floral notion of Victorian, and instead of the old jukebox a speaker in every corner blasting so loud you had to mouth.

She sat down on the dralon velvet and crossed those great legs and lit a fag, and I saw her hands were trembling.

She swigged her gin down in one. The record ended and there was sudden quiet as she slammed down the glass and said with force: 'I hated him.'

I said, 'Look.' And I told her all the things she would need to hear: how it's normal to feel anger when people go and die and leave you, and especially when, let's face it, however witty they've been and charming, they've also been a bad-tempered sod—you could hardly deny he'd got a lot to answer for, and there he'd gone without answering: he didn't exactly equip us, did he, to pick out decent men—here we sit, a broken marriage apiece and several messy affairs with women-hating bastards, the kind you come out of wrecked—her a smoker, and neither of us without our sticky moments over booze?

She said, 'But I loved him too,' and although the music had started up again, from the bitter violence with which she spoke there was no mistaking what she'd said. And huge tears were welling behind the contacts in those fantastic greeny eyes.

I said, 'Well, yes!' and said the other things, shouting against the music and recalling the positive; I said, Well, he had such a sense of adventure; he might have thought nothing of clipping us over the ear hole, but he thought everything of whisking us from our beds at dead of night to see the phosphorescence on the sea—though that time, I remember now, Lynne felt cold, which was perhaps why she couldn't recall it then in the pub. I said, he might have scowled, but he had a sense of humour; one thing, he gave us a healthy cynicism; I said: 'Especially you.'

She sobbed.

She shook her head. Her face was crumpled, her lips closed and stretched over those big teeth like Dad's in the photos before he got false ones. She put a finger up suddenly to the side of her face, holding it horizontally, the way she used to when she cried all those years ago. The tears dropped like rods past the polished dark wood into her lap.

And, against the music, she started talking. She told me about one day when she was five and we were all walking on the prom. Dad, as usual, was up ahead with his lips pursed and a fag cradled in his curled-up palm and turning it yellow. Lynne asked Mum, 'Why does Daddy never hold my hand?' Mum replied, 'Well go and ask him to!' (You can just see Mum: an act of faith, all falsely bright). Lynne ran and caught him up and asked. He raised his face, and had to focus, and then looked irritated and blank, and turned back grimly to his thoughts, and he hadn't even answered, leave alone taken hold of her hand.

I slid across the blue-grey dralon and put my arm round, and through the expensive perfume I could smell that old familiar musty smell of her that used to fill my nose when we lay in our double bed, taut and close and listening to Mum and Dad rowing downstairs. It had all gone wrong between them before Lynne was even born. When she was, it was no longer a happy family to be born into. Dad no longer waved to the toddler in dungarees in the garden, from the corrugated doors of the garage where he worked across the road. He had really already lost his belief in things and his sense of magic, or enough not to hand it on to the toddler playing in the garden, whose dungarees by then were hand-me-downs, and who by that time was Lynne. Enough not to give her a belief in herself.

She dipped to reach for a tissue, and I got a face-full of thick coarse hair, as I did when we used to fight. One time we fought beneath the bed—we were supposed to be dusting the lino, but we got into a row because she was making a play for one of my swotty boyfriends, and I was so mad I pinched her hard on the white flesh above her bloody sexy stocking tops, because I knew she didn't even want him, she just wanted to make me lose him. Besides, I was jealous, of her cool hard edges; I had only the vaguest inkling of the pain that had caused them, and I was envious, nevertheless. And she wanted to knock me off my pedestal, for being the lucky one, the one who'd ended up with the strength to offer a hand.

She blew her nose and all her high-lit curls bobbed, and it struck me suddenly that for all I knew she was starting to go grey.

She looked up and saw I was crying.

She sniffed and gave me a nudge. She said, 'Go on, get us another gin.'

Compass and Torch

The road ends at a gate. The boy waits in the car while the man gets out. Beyond the gate is the open moor, pale in the early evening with bleached end-of-summer grass, bruised here and there with heather and age-old spills of purple granite. The boy, though, is not looking that way, ahead. He is watching the man: the way he strides to the gate, bouncing slightly in his boots, his calf-muscles flexing beneath the wide knee-length shorts, the flop of hair at the front and the close-shaved neck as he bends for the catch.

The boy is intent. Watching Dad. Watching what Dad is. Drinking it in: the essence of Dadness.

The man pushes the gate with one arm, abruptly, too hard—the boy misses a breath—and sure enough, the gate swings violently, bounces off the stone wall and begins to swing back again while the man is already returning to the car. But then it slows, keels out once more, and comes to rest, wide open, against the wall: the man judged correctly after all. The boy is relieved. And, as the man drops into the driving seat something in the boy's chest gives a little hop of joy and he cries excitedly, 'Oh, I brought my torch!'

Coming downstairs after finding his torch, he overheard his mother say what she thought of the expedition.

Mad, she was calling it, as he knew she would. 'Mad! The first time in four months he has his eight-year-old son and what does he plan to do? Take him camping up a mountain! Talk about macho avoidance activity!' Her voice was low, and light and mocking, but he heard it catch, and he could also hear Jim, his mother's boyfriend who lived with them now, shifting at the kitchen table with an unhappy kind of rustle. His mother said: 'Well, what do you *expect*?' There was a choke in her voice now, and suddenly a kind of snarl: 'You wouldn't expect him to start *now*, would you—accommodating his child into his *life*?'

When the boy stepped into the kitchen he saw her start with alarm and shame. He said, 'I found my torch.'

'Oh good!' she said quickly, wrenching a look of bright enthusiasm onto her face.

The light seeping through her fuzzy hair made the bones of his shoulders ache.

Jim asked kindly, 'Is it all in working order?'

The boy forced himself to put the torch into Jim's big outstretched hand, to stand still and attentive while Jim gently twisted the barrel to make the bulb come on.

'It's a good one,' said Jim, pointedly approving, handing it back.

'Yes,' said the boy, forcing himself to acknowledge Jim's kindness and affirmation.

But Jim is not his dad.

'It's a red one,' he tells his dad now. 'It's in my rucksack.'

'Oh,' says his dad, 'good, good,' a little distractedly, driving the car quickly, efficiently through the gate. His dad parks the car neatly, gets out smartly and shuts the gate.

Some yards off on the tufted moor a scattered group of wild ponies lift their heads and sniff the air. One, dappled grey, moves with interest towards the car, man and boy.

The boy is still in the car, tugging at his rucksack, fighting with stiff straps to get at the torch. As the man comes back and puts his head into the open door, he holds it up: 'Here it is!'

'Great!' cries the man. He isn't looking at the torch.

He is looking away, seared by the glitter of anxiety in his little boy's eyes.

The horse comes up to the car. She nudges up, puts her nose over the edge of the door. The man bats her away.

It's OK, the boy decides, that his dad hasn't looked at the torch, hasn't studied or handled it like Jim. It's better: the torch is not for looking at now. It's better to have for it a proper purpose, to put it away, to carry it carelessly but with meaning, as a warrior might carry his sword. A torch is for lighting when the time comes, for lighting up the expedition of father and son.

'Come on!' says the man, all briskness now, and holds the door back for the boy to get out of the car.

Neither man nor boy takes much notice of the horse. The man steps back, and she swings her head out of the way. They go to the boot, and after a moment she slowly follows.

The boy is chattering:

'Have you brought one too, have you brought a torch?'

'Oh, yes!'

Is this a problem? the boy suddenly wonders. Does this make one of the torches redundant? For a brief moment he is uncertain, potentially dismayed, a mood which the man, for all his distraction, catches.

'We can use both of them, can't we, Dad?'

'Oh, yes! Yes, of course!'

Then a swoop of delight: 'We can light up more with both, can't we?'

'Oh yes, certainly!' The man too is gratefully caught on a wave of triumph. 'Oh, yes, two are definitely better! Back-up, for a start.'

Two torches are for lighting a bigger space in the wilderness, for lighting it together. Two torches are for father and son to back each other up.

The man has swung up the car-boot door. The horse, softly curious, is standing behind.

'What colour is your torch, Dad?'

'Er . . .' The man is peering into the boot, preoccupied once more now, turning his attention to the bags. 'Er . . . it's green.'

Unseen by the man and boy, clouds sweep like opening curtains above the brow of the hill and the grass lights up, bright yellow. Ancient rocks glint like heaving carcasses asleep.

Man and boy both peer intently into the boot. Behind them, the horse looks in too, through dark, deep-fringed eyes.

The man lifts up the tent in its smart holdall-style bag.

The boy still chatters. 'Is that the tent? What colour is it? Is it that round kind? Does it have a little porch?'

The man says with robust authority: 'It's an all-weather mountain tent. Two-man.'

The boy is thrilled. A tent to weather all conditions. In which he and his father will be two men.

The man looks up—for the first time—at the path they will take, which runs from the gate to the brow of the hill. Then he groans: 'I didn't bring a compass.'

The boy's eyes are suddenly wide with fear and dismay: not with the notion that they'll get lost, but because of the way the man's shoulders slumped and the tent in his hand dropped back onto the boot floor.

But then the man says quickly, almost brightly, 'Never mind!' and swings the tent out.

The boy breathes with relief. 'I've got a compass,' he cries, 'and guess what, I forgot mine too!'

He ought to have remembered it when he went upstairs for the torch. He might have thought of it if he hadn't already heard from his room the intent murmurings in the kitchen, and known the sort of thing his mother would be saying, and wanted badly to get back down there and make her stop.

No hope of him relating to his son on any personal, day-to-day level! No hope of him trying to RELATE to him, full stop!

The boy might have remembered it, the compass, as they were leaving. But he couldn't wait to get going, for it all to be over: the way his dad said, 'Hi there!' in that brittle, jovial way to Jim, and the way Jim dropped his eyes when he'd said Hi back, as if he understood all there was to understand about Dad, and didn't want to embarrass him by letting him know that. As if as well as despising him, Jim also—horribly—felt sorry for Dad.

And the way his mother said hardly anything, and made her face blank whenever Dad spoke to her or looked her way, and kept shredding a tissue so bits leaked though her fingers to the floor. When they were ready for off she put her head in through the car window, and her eyes were bulging and wobbly with tears, and he thought he couldn't bear this: that she didn't want him to go, that this moment which he had looked forward to, longed for, as his moment of joy, was a moment of unhappiness for her. And that terrible thing she had said then to Dad: 'Now you *will* be careful? Don't go camping too near the edge.' Unforgivable—as if she and Jim didn't think that Dad could think of such a thing for himself.

And then the worst thing of all: that brief but really awful moment when the car slid out of the drive and he felt, after all, he didn't want to go. That was another reason the compass never entered his head.

But they don't need a compass after all. They are adventurers, after all. Compasses are things that boys and dads tend to have, but which, when they are alert and strong at heart, they can leave behind. It is no accident that they both left their compasses behind.

'I keep mine by my bed,' he tells his dad. 'Where do you keep yours?'

'In my desk,' says the man.

The boy nods with satisfaction. He struggles unsuccessfully to get his arm in his rucksack strap; his arm flails.

The man notices this, and it makes his chest twist. He holds the strap wide so the boy can get his arm in. The horse nuzzles the rucksack top and the man pushes her away.

The horse sighs. She wheels around. Facing the open moor, she lifts her tail, spreads her hind legs and provides a close-up display which could easily fascinate an eight-year-old boy: opens and flexes her bright-red arse and lets out a steaming stream.

'Is it the kind of compass where the top lifts up, like mine?' asks the boy eagerly, with eyes only for the man.

As the stream goes on hitting the ground, the man snaps the boot shut, with satisfying clicks attaches sleeping bags and tent to his own pack, and shoulders the lot. The boy is gratified by his speed but unsettled by his subtle nervy hurry. The man checks the car locks. 'Right?' says the man decisively and, without looking round to check the boy is following, sets off.

Which is good, thinks the boy: no-nonsense. There's an important adventure ahead, which means there's no time for hanging around. 'Right!' he echoes, and sets off too, running to catch up.

Neither looks back at the nestled shiny car, the snaking wall, the ghost-coloured ponies in the hummocky grass.

The man strides; the boy walks fast, gladly half-runs, proud to keep up. They reach the top in no time. When they get there, they do not stop, as most walkers do, to take in the view, the purple sweep of the plain towards the blue wall of mountains beyond. They keep going, and the boy is asking, 'Is it one of those tents where you don't have to use pegs?'

Halfway down the next incline a thought suddenly occurs to the boy. He slows briefly, arrested. 'Dad, hey, do you think that horse wanted something to eat?'

'Maybe,' says the man, cheerfully, dismissively, having to call because the boy has fallen behind.

The boy puts his concentration into keeping abreast.

Ten minutes later, when the ponies reach the brow, heading in for the night, there is no sign on the plain of the man and the boy. Too purposeful to loiter, too focused on their goal to stop and gaze at the still black mirror of lake, man and boy have crossed the tract of land and are gone.

～

They camp under the highest peak, on the far side of the plain. They have pitched their tent, they have lit their stove, and in the quick-dropping dark at the foot of the mountain they have eaten their reconstituted soup. And all the time the boy talked: about the stove, about the valve at the top of its canister of gas—gabbling, his voice growing shrill when the man failed to light it first time and the flare sputtered and died.

In the plummeting darkness, the man's own anxiety began to mount. He could feel it gathering in the blackening chill: the aching certainty that already, only one year on from the separation, he has lost his son, his child. And the thought grew so strong that he could only half-listen to the child's earnest desperate voice.

At last the child, tucked up in his sleeping-bag, chattered himself out.

The man gently takes away the torch.

It isn't long before the man, already expert at blanking out pain, falls asleep too.

Neither hears the horses moving round the tent in the night.

For years to come, though, in his dreams the boy will see their wild fringed eyes and feel the deep thudding of their hooves.

Star Things

'There's things like stars in the stream.'

Angela Johnson nudges the gate.

'Come on,' says Angela Johnson, lolling her eyes about. Angela Johnson has socks that disappear down her sandals. She jumps on the gate and makes it swing inwards.

You should go straight home.

'Come and see the star things.'

My daddy's got a star thing, a thing called a meteorite, out of the sky.

At Angela Johnson's, when you call in the morning, there's a man sitting in the shadows who Angela Johnson ought in all decency not to call Daddy. Sunshine lops across the breathless dust of the sideboard and over the table, making bacon rinds oozy. The shadows around seem to wriggle. Angela Johnson's mother, still in her dressing gown, hardly says anything, and nothing at all about going straight home.

Angela Johnson's mother gets children while she's blinking.

Angela Johnson gets her clothes handed down. As she leans on the gate her dress that used to be her sister's goes up at the back and down at the front to her ankles.

'No one will know.'
The wood is black and yellow bars dipping over the hill crest.

No one knows where the Johnson children come from. No one knows where they go. Everyone knows what the business was their father went away on; some can guess why he broke down the back door with a hatchet.

In the wood there's something cracking.
Angela Johnson leaves the gate swinging. Down the hill there are boys, Johnson boys and others, breaking branches and slinging them. They jump, knees bent, swinging, till the whole tree winces; twigs and leaves spark and sizzle as they hurl them down the slope.
'Don't worry, no one will see.'

My daddy might come looking.
For children like the Johnsons the Social Services come looking. Children like the Johnsons have heads that are alive.
The boys come round, fists like pebbles in their pockets, legs in corrugated socks, their cropped hair bristling in the sun.
'Your dad's a Jew, then, isn't he?'

My daddy's got a star that fell out of the sky.
'What star? Hah!' Doubled up, snorting, kicking the tree trunks, throwing sticks looping upwards. 'Got a star, my eye!'
Yes, he has, he's got a meteorite he found while he was walking.
'You're joking, what's it look like?'
Split across, and in the middle there's a wheel shape all in silver.
Elbows leaning on the tree now. 'What's it made of?'

The meteorite lies in the glass-fronted cabinet. No one knows where it came from, no one knows what it's made of. Perhaps you better hadn't touch it.

Don't go too close to children whose bodies might be crawling. Don't let them get too near. Just in case, let's do your hair with a fine-toothed dust comb; scrub your nails and keep them short or you might catch worms.

'Your mam wears a hat, I seen her, and goes to church on Sundays.'

The Johnson children's mother wears a coat with half its buttons, no wonder when she's passing she turns her head as though she's wincing: you wonder really how she dares to walk abroad at all.

My daddy's got a star that fell while he was winking.

'What's the colour of the star, then?'

Once it was red-melting, but now it's black and silver.

'Ha!' Dancing off, sending currents of stone-flight out through the bracken: 'Her dad got bird shit in his eye!' Flicking back: 'What's it feel like?'

You're not supposed to know, remember, better hadn't touch it. Once it was on fire, but it must have been cooling when he put it in his pocket.

'So where did he find it?'

No one knows. No one knows how far he'd been when he walked abroad. And by the time he brought it home it had gone stone cold.

And weren't there lots of questions? And didn't someone call out in the night time? And then they made the rule about the glass-fronted case.

Now the boys are off, lolloping, spinning sticks at blackbirds to make them go cack-crackling, looking for a spot that's flat enough for marbles.

Angela Johnson's tugging: 'Let's go to the stream.'

The sun's getting lower, the air fizzing with midges, flicking on and off in pinpoints. Baubles of stained sunshine smash across the ground.

One of the Johnsons has a scar across his forehead.

Johnson children get dropped from their prams.

'What's the meteor's shape?'

Like a chopped-off finger, a knobbly knuckle.

The Johnson boy's scar jumps like forked lightning: 'Ha! Someone threw her dad a knuckle bone!'

My mummy's got a scar that she covers up with powder. Powdered skin is sweet and dry, has a perfume that lingers after someone's gone to church. Be careful near the dressing table, all those bowls and cut-glass bottles: scent that's been spilled stains the polished surface, and powder makes a breathless cloud . . .

Angela Johnson slithers off down the tussocks. Golden kingcups in the water, oily with the sunshine.

Stars that ooze and bubble from the mud that you could slip on.

You can slip on the mud and badly scar your cheekbone, lose your hat and scar your cheekbone; run through mud with a pushchair, banging, slipping on the grass slope, suddenly tumbling backwards, wheels upended, spinning. You'll be lying cheek down, sobbing: there's no getting away, you can't undo the mistake you made.

Now the boys come swaggering, lice in their heads and wriggling worms inside their bellies, throwing pebbles, knocking kingcups, punching holes in the water.

Don't throw stones.

Don't throw anything.

Don't throw powder bowls and bottles . . .

'Hey, here's your dad, here's the Jew!'

Run, and the sun's clip-clipping the branches; nearer: light slicing the grasses; grasp his knuckles: it's so late, the way home now has different shadows.

My daddy's got a star that hit the earth and died.

Leaf Memory

This is the memory:

Down below is a brown, dry stream. It swishes. One long unbroken swish: that's the wheels; and slumph-slumph: that's Nanny's feet. I put my arm over the side—bluish-black, with a bright white line that slides along slyly when I move my head. I lean right over. I put my hand down into the stream, and the dry bits tickle.

'Put your hand in,' says Nanny.

I sit back on the cushions.

Nanny's hands are on the handle. Between them, another line of light winks and glares.

The dry things swish.

One gets stuck in a wheel. Clutter-clutter. I look over. It whips, round and round. It flickers on the others.

Where do they come from?

'From up,' says Nanny.

The trees are up. Up there it is green, green-and-black against the sky.

'They fell off,' says Nanny. 'The brown ones fell off.'

She is starting to puff. Now we've begun to go up the hill. I slide forward. My feet press on the bottom.

Crackle-crackle in the wheels. The colour of burn. The burnt ones fell off.

The burnt bits are down.

'Get your hand in,' says Nanny.

We are halfway up the hill.

And then I see, after all, some trees have gone down. Tree tops lower than her waist.

And my nanny is walking on the rim of the world.

This is family history:

She had six of us grandchildren. She pushed me up the hill to see my newborn baby sister.

In the memory, she is taller than trees.

She is big, her jaws wobble. Her hands are round the handle. Crackle-crackle in the wheels.

'Get your hand in,' she says, 'you are big enough to know better.'

I am big. She is biggest.

But I am bigger than I was.

Now there is somebody smaller than me.

We go under the trees.

Dark splotches dive into the pram and swoop out again.

The hill is steeper. She bends over to push and her wobbling jaws come down to join her hands.

'You are a weight,' she says. She is puffing. 'Your weight is something.'

I am heavy. I am bigger. But I need to be pushed. She can push. The brown bits swish. Dark splotches swim across her face and hands.

Where do they come from?

'From the trees.' The brown bits are down, and dark smudges are flying, coming off the trees.

Down below and behind is a bright green hole filled with tree-top cushions. My nanny's heels are kicking the tops of the trees.

The pram was old. She had used it previously for her own children.

We come out into the sun again. The black smudges shoot off. The pram sides light up, dusty blue. Nanny's dark dress fades. The cloth glimmers as she moves. The sun burns my legs. In the wheel a dry bit crackles.

Now her hands on the pram are stretched and shining.

They have faint brown blotches.

Look, the shadows have left marks.

'Oh aye,' says Nanny, 'they're the marks of growing old.'

We have come through the trees.

She is older.

I am bigger.

She clenches tight, pushing the pram to the peak of the world.

She wasn't young when she married. Her husband was younger, the quiet, shamefaced son of a drunkard. She bore him four children. She pushed her children round in the big blue pram.

More brown bits get caught. Tack-tack.

I lean over to see.

'Don't lean over,' says Nanny.

We reach the top. She stops the pram. She straightens up to get her breath. Her face floats up away from her hands. Something winks on her front. Brooch. She keeps it in a box at the side of the bed. Her bed. And Grandpa's. Grandpa throws me up: God, you're a weight.

My weight is something.

We are tall, and resting on the peak of the world.

He wasn't like most men. Teetotal, industrious. And good with the children. She loved that husband.

She looks down and round at the dry bits in the wheel. She stoops, her head drops below the side of the pram. She keeps hold with one hand. One hand on the handle. I lean over to watch. Her hair is parted and caught in a brown thing. Comb. She keeps it with the brooch. Along the parting I can see the skin of her head has shadowy blotch-marks. One mottled hand

and her head jerk below the pram side. The pram rocks, I hold the sides.

'Don't lean over,' she says. 'You'll tip. Your weight is something.'

I am something.

I am bigger. I am bigger than the baby.

I wait, high in my pram, while she clears the wheels on the rim of the world.

Few could have hoped to make such a blessed marriage. Her daughters could hardly expect to be so lucky. But they loved their men.

She stands. She is puffing.

She says, 'We'd better get on. Your mam will be sending your dad out to find us.'

My daddy throws me, up towards the ceiling, and then I am falling . . .

My nanny's hands go up behind her head. She pushes the comb in. Her stomach bulges round the handle.

The pram jerks, and then she is running. Everything slips; something sweet and sharp is pulling in my tummy. Her hair flies out from her forehead, all the wispy bits escaping.

Her comb slips out and is gone, a brown bit fallen down the side of the world.

She had four children. Three survived.

Next in the memory, her hand is on the door. She holds me to her. I am tucked beneath her bulges. She smells sweetish-sour. Her blotchy hand pushes the wood and makes an opening. My mummy's voice curls through it.

'Come on in, come on, where are you?'

In the room it is dim.

My mummy sits in the bed. Her knees are up, like a mountain. There is something on her face.

She says, 'Here's your baby sister.'

What is that that's on her face?'

My nanny steers me over. She says, 'See, your baby sister!'

Along my mummy's cheek is a big brown blotch thing. She smiles, the brown thing twitches.

She says, 'It's just a little burn.'

My mummy looks at my nanny. She says, 'It's the ether, the mask slipped.'

My nanny lifts me past the mountain: 'See, there's your baby sister.'

My nanny nods at my mummy.

She had four childbirths of her own. The fourth was a stillbirth.

That is all; after all there are no men in the memory. Just my mummy's face with its stark burnt leaf; the dark flake of the baby lying over the mountain, over the edge of the world beside her; and my nanny, her shadowed hands in her lap, folded and fallen.

A Glossary of Bread

BREAD: *From Old English, in turn from Old Frisian,* **brēad** (OED), *originally meaning* **morsel**, *or* **crumb** (Clark Hall's Concise Anglo-Saxon Dictionary, 1966).

∾

ROLL: *A small individual loaf of bread, properly one rolled or doubled over before baking* (OED).

Rolls. This is what we call them nowadays, any miniature loaf of any consistency or shape—a generic label on supermarket shelves everywhere in an age of mass distribution and multinational food corporations, the old specific local names deleted or displaced as national retail specialities. It's what Janey and I now call the soft round ones we are buttering for our father's funeral.

Time dissipates the meanings.

I lever them open and smear their yielding white insides. Janey folds them closed again on ham, which throughout our childhood our father banned from the house, but gave in and ate in the end.

The clock ticks on the wall, time catching in the throat.

We used to call them call them *baps,* says Janey, but we can neither of us remember where this was or when.

BAP: *First recorded use late 16th century, origin unknown.* ***A small loaf or roll of baker's bread of various sizes and shapes in different areas*** (OED, 1933); ***a large soft bread roll*** (Shorter OED, 1993)

Was it Rhyl? Where we landed up in the early fifties, too young at the time to think of them as *the post-war years?* We had left a world of green where the past looked out of framed photos with faces that were familiar and which people told us were like our own. The place of our grandparents, our mother's parents. Our mother's world.

Here where our father had brought us, there was concrete and neon. Here we didn't know a soul. Here was being adrift and knowing not just the strangeness of everything around you, but that of your own. Our father's world.

Here our mummy didn't go to church any more, not simply because she didn't want to, we guessed. Her smile was brittle. Daddy was brooding and silent. There was darkness, brown paint and shadow in our flat above the baker's, and harsh buffeting light on the flat breathless prom. A scary height from our window to iron pavement below.

This was the place where we started to cringe.

We waited with our baby brother's pram while Mummy went into the baker's. Piled up in the window were baps, if that was what we called them then: forbidden, too expensive for us, for people like us (though there weren't any other people adrift and inexplicably uneasy like us). Nothing for what they cost, mere crumbs. But not nothing: delicate drops, golden, dusted with flour, promising softness and warmth. Our mouths watered. We leaned our foreheads on the glass.

And then Mummy came out again carrying the loaf in its bag of cellophane with its ready-cut slices which tasted rubbery and cold, her smile too bright. 'Come on!' she cried, too brightly, and stuffed the loaf in the pram where it squashed and then bounced back again into shape, 'Let's go for a walk on the prom!'

And set off, and we followed, and her blue silk dress, handed down from a better-off aunt, lifted up and shivered in the agitated air, then flapped around my legs as I kept up at the side.

Bap. A plump word, a word with softness, but also the sound of something tapping. Did we take it there with us from the safer place we had left, an old English word from a comfortably anglicised vale of Wales, or did we pick it up then, like one of the pebbles thrown up by the storms onto that concrete-strangled Celtic shore?

BARA. The Welsh word for bread. We never took it on our tongues, which we'd stopped with our thumbs. We sat dumb in the lessons. In the evenings we were speechless and stilled as music outside sobbed from the arcades and we waited in fear for Daddy to come home.

And then suddenly, unexpectedly, we moved again, to a town in the English Midlands where the bread rolls went by a different name. Was this the place where they called them *buns*?

BUN: Late Middle English, origin unknown. A small soft round sweet bread or cake with currants (Shorter OED, 1993). *Possibly from the Old French bugne, meaning a swelling produced by a blow* (OED, 1933).

There were boys who threw stones because of how we spoke. We ducked the stones, we learnt to hear our own accents as strange, our names for things as alien and archaic, and quickly spat them out, forgot them, as no longer our own.

We were as foreign to our father as he was to us, with his silence, the mere crumbs of his history, the distant land of his birth he hardly ever mentioned, his failure to bequeath us a sense of continuity or belonging.

His eyes would glitter at us blankly. He would stay away for days and then the lights of his car returning up the drive would throw shadows like swooning bodies down the hall wall.

In the sparse cold house, we would come into the kitchen and find our mother bent over at the table weeping.

Somewhere else we lived, they called them *cobs*.

COB: Late Middle English, implying 'rounded' or 'head'. Origin unknown. A round-headed loaf (Shorter OED, 1993).

He hit me on the head, caught me a stinging blow on the ear. He was lashing out now, unpredictable, uncontrolled.

We kept away. We ran the streets, the blackened terraces of ports and mining towns, the tumbling tenements of a Scottish city; we joined the gangs, learnt the street games, sucked on sweets in the insular raucous haven of street-light glow, gobbled up the catchwords of each new place like chameleons snatching flies. Stayed out as long as possible, knowing that the longer we did, though, the more likely we'd be to get the stinging slipper or the biting cane or the burning snapping belt.

COB: Meaning also **to strike on the buttocks with an instrument, as a punishment.** *Nautical, mid-eighteenth century.*

To crush or bruise. *Industrial, late eighteenth century.*

Also: to get a cob on: **to become angry.** *Slang, mid-twentieth century, origin unknown.* (Shorter OED, 1993).

Whichever place it was we lived where they used the word *cob*, the term was specific, meaning precisely not a soft but a hard-crusted roll.

We got hardened. We got clever.

Muffins they called them in Glasgow. 'Do you want a muffin?' a new friend's mother asked me, and though I expected something like a crumpet (Shorter OED 1993: *MUFFIN: a flat circular spongy cake of bread often eaten toasted*), I didn't miss a beat when she handed me a plain bread roll. I was coming to revel in overturnings of the standard definitions, in the interchangeability of terms: the word *bap* turning up again, not this time as a name for small rolls but for the large flat breads which in yet another place were called *oven bottoms*. I loved the subversion of generic confusions, the fact that in some places bread rolls were called *cakes*.

Barmcakes, they called them, in that flat Midlands town where I finally rebelled.

BARM: from Old English, probably in turn from Low German, **beorma:** *the froth on the top of fermenting malt liquor; yeast* (Shorter OED, 1993).

BARMY: full of ferment (OED, 1933).

I was twelve and full of ferment, fizzing with possibilities, with a sense that no definition or state of affairs was ever set in stone, that all realities could shift, be challenged. I challenged him: jumped like a lizard out of the way so he flailed the air, answered back from a safer distance while he stood there wild, *barmy,* and though it meant I'd get a worse beating in the end, I was high with a sense of reality new-coined.

I said (hardly flinching) that I wanted to go to chapel. I didn't really, but a boy I fancied had invited me, and I was challenging all of my father's hegemony, which included, I had always thought, a ban on our mother's religion.

He didn't snap. He scowled, but he didn't bristle or glare.

Time dissipates the meanings. No definition or state of affairs is ever set in stone.

He said he wouldn't stop me.

I felt triumphant. I knew I looked it, and contemptuous. I saw him see it, and look away. His shoulders slumped.

He looked back up, his eyes white-hot. He said carefully, bitterly, almost sarcastically, that the last thing he'd ever wanted to do to me was blight my life over religion, the thing that had once been done to him.

Yiddish: **broyt,** *from Old High German* **brōt.**

~

BREAD: a word which has passed from its original meaning **broken piece or pieces** *through the sense of* **'piece of bread'** *into that of* **bread as a substance** (OED, 1933).

BREAD: The means of subsistence (OED 1993).

Going Back

Then they came out onto a plain.

A man, and a woman carrying a bundle, and a child in red wellingtons with a bucket and spade, who kept lagging behind.

Before, they had been walking in a soft green lane of English countryside, just before; feathers of plantain and dot-balls of daisies and broad cushions of shoulder-high birch trees. And the child in red wellingtons kept lagging. And now and then the man got ahead, unwittingly carried by his longer stride, and after a while he would stop, and wait for them, and when the woman got level he would ask, Are you all right . . . all right? Shall I carry the baby now? She would shake her head and hug the baby to her. She was breathless, and heavy down through all her limbs, but she would carry on a little while yet . . .

All right . . . Are you really all right?

They turned and called the dawdling child, and lingered, and then went on again. And so they emerged from the soft green lane, and came out onto a plain.

What is this? asked the child.

What is this place called?

And he stood stock-still staring at the vista.

It is a place, said the man, where the sea once came.

They were standing in a shallow blue-grey bowl. The child looked around, and then searched his parents' faces.

He asked, Where has it gone?

Gone. Gone . . . Something has gone . . .

And then he remembered how **of course** *it had been: the bowl rocking wetness, and light convoluted; eel ribbons flickering, movement endless as memory, and substance solvent as a dream.*

And he placed his foot gingerly, and for one moment he was giddy . . .

They did not know the vegetation. The varieties were specialized, and the hues did not seem natural. A creeping plant, some kind of sea-bred bramble, clamped the earth. Blue-black. Mutant.

Cloudberries, said the man, picking at the fruits of it, though he knew it was not quite the same.

Cloudberries, he said, to give the plant a name.

Can you eat them? asked the boy.

Best not, said the woman.

Can I eat them? He repeated.

The woman had gone.

And where was the sea?

Not that way, said the man, pointing to a clot of firs. They must lead away from the higher vegetative colonization; they must follow the petering to primitive grasses. They bore to their left. On the mother's chest the baby curled like a padded fold of skin. Still he slept, but her breasts leaked milk already. They must get to the beach before it was time, and the baby woke. The woman swallowed, and her throat felt thick.

And the man turned, and said, Here, let me have him–and relieved his wife, four weeks past her labour, of her burden.

And so they reached the brow of the ridge.

And they had been wrong. Away in front of them stretched acres of woodland. They had come the wrong way. They must wheel away again, bear to their right. After all they must pass the dark smudge of firs.

Eager now to find the right direction, the man stepped out, making for the fir trees, his bundle no burden, leaving the other two way behind.

And now the woman found her arms flapped, swung away heavily, now they had no bundle; she had lost her compactness, and thus her forward motion. She took the free hand of the wellingtoned child, and he stared around, and dragged, and pulled her backwards.

Away in front, under the trees, her husband stopped.

Come on, he shouted, come on, but the words were lost in the intervening distance. She watched his mouth opening and shutting, and the black-green land rolled and spread itself out between them.

She moved her legs.

You must feed the baby, said her husband.

You must. Must.

Feed the baby. Want to feed the baby. Must want.

Yes, she wants. Breasts taut and shiny. Glistening with tension. Wants relief.

But must undo buttons. Pull, tug. Peel wet clothing. Wrench, fix.

The baby squealed its subterranean squeal. Her husband said kindly, Sit on this log.

She fed the baby. The man and the boy drifted away.

The child followed his father.

He said, Why don't we go? Why don't we get there?

We must wait, said the man.

And the boy plucked the hard blue stuff of his father's tall trousers, and said again, Why don't we go?

The baby sucked. Flat face clamped, jaws and tongue rippling rhythmically. And her milk flowed, and her breasts became easier, and her body sank back to that old aching sleepiness, and looking around her now she saw in the grass strange yellow poppies that grew only here, nowhere else in the land, pale opaque bubbles floating on the green.

The man came back to get the baby. She tucked it up and handed it back.

He asked, Do you want to go on yet?

Each time he remembered about how she felt: recognised the signs she gave, acknowledged the causes, was familiar with the ways to help. But he could not know her feeling. He could not feel her knowing. He took the baby. To touch the spring of contact, he handled their baby.

It lay in his arms like a satisfied leech.

Can you go on?

Can you? Can I . . . go on?

She lugged her breasts back into her cold sodden clothes. They went on.

And the child began running. Now! Now we will get there! And his legs felt buoyed, and the air glanced away from his slick-rushing arms . . .

. . . and he knew this too, he knew the sweet bubbling . . .

. . . and even the woman felt able to hurry . . . and the land opened out into deep undulations, grass swathes swishing, a green roller-coaster . . .

And then the ground in front of them was gone.

Gone. Space before them.

They stopped, each in turn, teetering. The woman reached out for the hand of the child.

What is it? asked the child.

The land scoured deep, sheer with smooth damp sand. Falling sharply several-score feet and then rising again all around. Away on the left there was no fringe of grass but a flip of bright sand at the lip of the down-rushing slope.

She thought, That's where the sea comes in.

And she thought, We could fall.

> I could fall
>> He could fall
>>> And the sea would come rushing . . .

She stepped back.

She pointed to the left. She said to her man, That way lies the sea.

No, no. Not at all. He said. To the right lies the sea.

He said. See the light. Feel the air.

Not moving off yet, they stood at the edge.

Ah yes! thought the boy: roly-poly, pell-mell, this is it, hush-rush.

And the woman gave in, for she did not care to bother, and turned to go the way her man thought best.

And the boy in red wellingtons went forward to step off the edge.

And the man could say: He would not have hurt.

Say it, simply. Not have hurt. Would not.

I'd have shuffled down and brought him back.

Shuffled down, dig-slip, puffs of sand. Brought him back.

But what, she thought with a wild slip of thinking, what if they couldn't get back before the tide came rushing in?

But the tide was right out.

After all, her husband had been right. The sea was his way, the way he said. The land sloped gently, and the sand was like salt, dug and sifted in piles by sharp blue-grass combs.

And the sea was a long way out.

And the beach was damp, like tacky urban clay. Across the bay a land mass lowered.

The man and the boy went down on the beach to play. The woman crouched back, at the edge of the dunes. She thought, I could not go to where they are. I could not churn on that wet sand-clay. I could not bear the ridges on the soft little pads of my toes. I will stay, like a lizard on the edge of the dunes.

Over the estuary, the land mass oozed from out of the horizon. A city peninsula, like volcanic detritus.

And the boy had forgotten—yes, really quite forgotten—this empty breathless feeling . . .

The beach was not what they had hoped for, or expected. The sand grew hulks that had spored from the city, the bulk of a door half-buried in the seaweed line, a grainy baker-boy hat, a curling black-hand glove. Stiffened, grainy, they became of the element.

And so the element was altered.

Two inches down the man and the boy dug up oil.

They dug, and made streaky, oily castles.

And the man could say, simply, Nonsense.

Nonsense. The sea would never come up there.

But the sea could sweep round . . .

Nonsense. Simply. Why, the sea does not go past the edge of the dunes.

But the dunes are ripped open, and the sand is scored cleanly.

And quite damp.

The boy came running. I need to shit. Need to. Must. You must. Must see to him. Must dig him a hole. Must pull down his trousers, expose his white flesh. Wait. And then cover. Cover the hole, and dress up his bottom.

She thought, I am tired.

I am tired of pushing and pulling, and peeling and tucking.

To push just once, let go, and not to have to push again...

But she thought, I could fall

> fall
>> fall, fall
>>> and the tide would come rushing . . .

She sat back on the sand. She crouched on the land.

The man and the boy went off again and left her.

And now the baby had woken with the changing of hands and all the commotion, and was crying, and either she must stand and walk to rock him to sleep again, or she must feed him once more.

She pulled out her breast and stuffed the rubber of the nipple in the round black hole of his mouth.

Man and boy, where had they gone?

Gone?

She slewed her vision. Yes, there they were, in the same place as before. There, where they'd puckered and rucked up the sand. But when she'd looked up she had missed them. As though the vista had shifted.

The baby's mouth slackened in sleep on her breast. She prised him away.

Away at their digging, the man and boy waved.

She thought, something is wrong.

Pink sand, bluish grass, sky getting yellowy.

What was wrong?

There was no pervading, no prevailing tone. The planes did not harmonize. Blue split from yellow, yellow cracked away from pink. The spectrum was broken. Man and boy, little dolls, balanced on the surface of it. It could tip

They could fall

        through the cracks
          off the edge

          tip and fall

She stood up suddenly and called the boy.

The man and the boy looked up and noticed her, the woman mouthing and waving at the edge of the dunes.

Time to go, thought the man, knowing what was best for them.

Time for tea, thought the boy.

All right, said the man, go ahead, the tide is coming in now—and pushed the boy—your mother's calling.

Ah yes, thought the boy, it's going back's the best thing, time for tea!

Red wellingtons flashed off across the sand.

The man bent down to gather up the spade and bucket, and the flakes of seashells the boy had been collecting.

When he straightened up his wife and child had gone.

Gone.

What has gone?

His mother's hand was a claw on his arm. She pulled, and his feet kept slipping.

Why are we rushing? Where are we going?

She didn't answer. She yanked him on. His armpit hurt, and his ankles turned, feet scooping in the salty crumble. In silence she pulled.

All right?

Is it all right?

And this was the feeling the boy had not had, the one he had not known before.

The boy was getting frightened now.

He fell and was dragged.

Where were they? Leaping, then slipping, the man could not find them. Going back, the way was much harder. Hiding the view now, the dunes seemed much deeper.

He called. Where were they?

He called again.

Red legs flailing, the child hung and flapped like a feathery prawn.

The tide could sweep round.

They could
        could fall
            fall and tumble
                tumble-fall

She would prove it.
    One day she would push
        and have done.

Into The Night

A different city, washed clean as a beach by the light of early evening in spring.

She's far from home.

As she steps from the railway station, pigeons rise up before her, wheel in a thrill of flight over pink-tinged buildings, then sink back down with a breathing of wings like a sigh.

She crosses the city towards the reception, and the day falls softly around her, gives in.

The room's in underwater gloom, the conversation a muted bubble. The last rays of the sun slice the dense space and make red-gold ripples on the floor. Mid-sentence, she looks up across the cave of the room, and is caught on the hook of a stranger's white eyes.

As the line between them pulls, she feels him unbalance too, his tanned features freeze yet soften, his tall frame tense yet give in, his command of conversation falter.

He looks away quickly, to save himself.

She looks away too.

But she knows he doesn't want to be saved.

She waits, tingling with awareness of her image which has caught him, the slick of black fabric over her fluid limbs, her fall of glittering hair, the mole on her neck like a magic sign.

She could save herself now, turn her back. But she won't.

She's at a table with others when he comes.

She doesn't look up. She knows without looking—she has grasped it already in that one first glance—the controlled tender grace with which he lifts the chair one-handed; she hears the small careful tap as he places it back on the floor before sitting. He speaks to her neighbours, but she knows without looking that all his attention, all the urgent message in his light but careful voice, is for her.

And then her neighbour is asking him, Has he met her, does she know him, and there's the naming of names, there's the need to look at his face.

She allows her gaze to travel as far as his mouth. A big mouth, generous, large teeth which he reveals in a smile then suddenly covers, pursing his lips, understanding the need not to give too much away.

She drops her eyes, and her gaze alights on his hand. A large hand, loosely cupped on the table. The fingers tinged nicotine-yellow. He speaks, explaining some point, and his hand draws a circle in illustration. It comes towards her, circling, huge and full of potential power, but cupped in supplication and yellow-stained. It circles away again, pulling on the invisible line between them, tugging on her nipples and groin.

As they leave together half an hour later they have spoken less than a score or so words. They go down the stairs without speaking. Side by side, but not touching, they step out into the night.

It's dark now in the city. Sirens ache across the vacuum reaches, neon bleeds into the distance like moonlight on the sea. Above, a phosphorescent glow hides the other-worlds of stars.

He touches her now, takes her arm to pull her, dodging, between the streaming traffic. He keeps hold. Now they are touching, their bodies weakening. Now they hurry.

They stumble alone into the lift of his hotel, two strangers, two points of pure desire coming together, pure body, yellow-stained hands mapping breasts beneath the black fabric, parting her thighs, jutting cock clamped in her fist, their particular personal histories washed away by their blinding bathing mouths. He shuts the door of his room, shuts it on the city, on all that each of them was before this moment, this night; entangled, tearing at clothes, they move towards the bed, tripping briefly on something, some possession which might define him, which he kicks deftly out of the way. They arc towards the bed's surface, and all of their pasts is tongued, licked, sucked from their bodies, chased to the base of her spine, flicked from her nipples, her cunt, drowned with his cock in the lagoon of her mouth and the liquid delta between her thighs, lost altogether in the widening rings of their orgasms.

~

She wakes to a line of morning light between the curtains. On the floor, the light picks out an object, the thing he kicked away. His suitcase, holding his belongings, holding the evidence of his life.

At her back, he breathes, still sleeping.

She doesn't turn.

She could get up now, quietly, without waking him. She could dress silently and quickly, without turning around. She could grab her bag and cross the room without looking back, go through the door and shut it behind her. She could leave it behind her, her erotic encounter, simple and pure and intact.

Or she could turn, examine properly his sleeping face. She could wait till he wakes. And for the histories to surface which impelled them together, she to a man with his fingers stained by addiction, he to a woman with the mark of a mole on her neck and a pell-mell plunge of waterfall hair.

She waits, undecided. The light between the curtains sharpens and the shape on the floor gathers definition.

Conundrum

They were children of the 1950s, this girl and boy, they were punished, even beaten, as a matter of course, just for making mistakes, or for simply not knowing, indeed for being their innocent childhood selves.

But they were children of the 1960s, too: they rebelled.

They met at a student demonstration, though when the protest got violent they left together, they refused to fulfil the pop-psychology notion that victims inevitably become aggressors in the end. Like Christ and Mohammed, they resisted the impulse to revenge.

They wore flowers. They joined CND, they embraced the idea of unilateral disarmament, they chained themselves to airbase fences, they blew kisses at the cops who rough-handled them away.

They applied to the world the philosophy of forgiveness their parents had failed to apply to them.

They settled down. They had a child, and brought to childcare the lessons they'd learnt.

Above all what they wanted was a child who felt cherished as they hadn't.

They knew that empathy was the key to this goal.

Unlike their parents who had ignored them as crying babies, they understood their baby's cries as expression of a genuine need. Indeed, as he screamed, as he threw his toddler tantrums, as, ten years old, he wanted bigger better toys, or, a teenager, more expensive gear, they relived their own childhood feelings of hurt or deprivation, and hastened in desperation to quell them in him and fulfil his needs.

When he swore in their faces, though, they were shocked. They were devastated too when he stole from their wallets and in anger kicked their doors down. When the cops picked him up for violent, even fascist behaviour, when the social worker pronounced him deeply troubled, well, they couldn't believe it, or imagine where on earth they could have gone wrong.

The Way to Behave

Sisterhood, it's just a wonderful thing.

After all, who do you turn to when your husband's unfaithful with another woman, but the woman herself?

I ring the doorbell.

Dark-brown-painted door with frosted panels of early-twentieth-century glass, giving nothing away. A small bay-windowed terrace. Tiny front garden, neat and non-committal with herbs and crazy paving. A single elder casting shadows like a jigsaw puzzle. A suitable home for a woman living alone.

I've no doubt she's single.

I know she's blonde, I found the hair on his jacket, my first proof, talk about pushing me into a cliché.

Of course he denied it, talk about treating a woman with contempt.

The garden slumbers behind me in the autumn sun.

She won't keep me waiting, she knows I'm coming.

I know her voice. This morning, early, she rang the house for the very first time. The sound came through the dawn, through the shrouded rooms and through my dreams, bubbles of it rising from the hall below, the sound of alarm and warning. The sound of guilt and also of plea. I knew straight away, before I'd woken fully, it was the sound I'd been waiting for. A sound being rung for me, not him.

He slept on, foolish man, mobile switched off beside him, hammocked in his complacency and time-honoured male code of divide and rule, a baby glow above his beard.

I got up, made my way down the shadowed stairs, picked up the receiver, the noise ripping, the plug pulled on the secret.

'Hello?'

There was a horrified silence; then: 'Can I speak to Ian?'

She sounded panicked—she must be having some sort of crisis—but there was also curiosity, and abandoned relief.

I didn't need to ask, *Who is this? . . . At this time of the morning?* I side-stepped the stereotype and simply laid down the receiver and went and roused him and watched the games-up alarm in his opening pale-blue eyes.

I could have killed him, though, for the smoothness with which he changed his expression, sauntered down the stairs with his social-worker's calm, came back and swung his lithe pale legs into his trousers, rolling his eyes about a crisis with a client.

He either thinks I'm a fool or he counts on me wanting to believe him, and who's the bigger fool there, I'd like to know?

He was going down the path when I dialled 1471.

She hadn't withheld her number.

She was at home when I rang her, after I knew he'd be gone to work.

I couldn't help it, I was still so angry, I asked roughly: 'Are you the woman who's trying to grab my husband?'

Another silence filled with horror. Then she said in pain, 'Look. *He* has to be responsible, surely, for his own actions. I'm very fed up with the way he's treating us both, keeping us both in the dark all the time!'

I have to admit I was taken aback. I was silenced a moment. Then: 'Look, can we meet?'

In a rush of relief she cried, 'Oh yes, I think we *should!*'

'Can I come there?'

Alarm. Tentative: 'Well, don't you think we should meet on neutral territory?' And then before I could answer: 'Oh no, of course not, I'm being stupid, that's the language of war, it's not the way to behave! Of course you can come here!'

She moves up behind the frosted panes, the door opens.

She's young, I should have known, her blond hair in a plait down her back, he always promised he'd never do that, run off with a younger woman, men simply don't know themselves.

She leads me in, looking stricken, compassionate and yet confessional. She invites me to sit in her little front room, yellow with morning sun and sparse with junk-shop furniture.

'You're single?' I ask her.

'Divorced.'

To my shock, I notice children's books on the shelves. 'You've got *children*?'

'Two. Seven and four.'

She pauses. 'Mark, the four-year-old, he's not well, he's asleep upstairs. He had a fever this morning and I couldn't get a doctor. I was very frightened.'

She's looking at me carefully. 'Ian had always told me I must ring if anything like that happened. This time I did.'

I'm silent, taking all this in. At last I say: 'You called his bluff.'

A wry understanding passes between us.

I say bitterly, 'Men are like babies. They want it all ways.'

She cries in a rush of agreement, 'I *know*!'

'Like to think they're heroes, and all they are are cowards!'

'Oh yes!'

'Relying on us women always to be too frightened to rock the boat!'

'Exactly!'

In spite of all the pain, there's a feeling now of relief, and comradeship even, in the yellow-sun-filled room.

I can't help saying though, 'But don't you think it's immoral, taking advantage, taking someone else's husband?'

She's upset again. 'I don't want to *take* him!'

She sees my look. 'No, no *really*! It has to be up to him! He has to make his own choices. He has to choose, he can't go on keeping us both in misery like this!'

'Keeping his bread buttered both sides.'

'Quite! And honestly'—she's leaning forward, intent and serious—'I haven't wanted to deceive you. I've *hated* it! The secrecy, it's so demeaning: for me, and for you! I have begged him to tell you and put us out of our misery. Even if it means I lose him.' She pauses. 'Because, actually, from where I'm standing it's clear he wants to protect his marriage to you at all costs.'

Her creamy face is thrust forward, tragic and brave.

This gives me food for thought, I have to say.

'Yes,' I say. 'He needs to grow up, face up to what he's doing and choose.'

I add, cynical, 'But do we want him now?'

She gives a little sad laugh. We both laugh. The warm sun fills the room. It's almost as if he's written himself out of the equation, it's between me and her now.

'After all,' I say, 'his feet stink.'

'Oh yes, they do!'

'And he's so untidy. He leaves his stuff all over.'

'Oh, I know! He's always leaving plastic bags full of things lying about!'

'And you can't take him anywhere, he's got no social graces.'

'That's very true!'

We laugh again.

Our laughter fades. There's a rueful silence. I break it: 'You don't have a cup of coffee, do you?'

'Oh, of course!' And she rushes off to the kitchen, full of guilt at not having thought of it before, and glad of another way of bridging things between us.

I look around. I realize suddenly why the room is so yellow.

She comes back with the coffee. I say, 'This is my yellow carpet isn't it?'

She's riveted. 'Oh god! He said it was *his*! I mean, even then, I didn't want to accept it, something out of your house . . . But then . . . He said it was up in the attic and not needed, and that *you* hardly knew of its existence . . . And well, it was so cold in here and my kids kept getting ill . . . ' She crumples in her chair. 'Oh, I do feel awful.'

'It's okay,' I say quickly. 'Yes, I'd forgotten all about it.' But I can't stop myself saying, 'And that's my blue bowl sitting there on top of your TV.'

She almost dies. 'He said you'd thrown it out! And I really badly didn't want it here, but after all it was his, I mean he's brought so many things he's practically half moved in . . . And if I'd thrown it out too it would be like trashing *you*, trashing his relationship with you, which as I say was the last thing I wanted to do! So I just couldn't touch it and left it there.'

She half-collapses. 'It's so *complicated*, this situation he's put us in . . . '

'Don't worry,' I say, 'I had thrown it out.'

She looks unnerved.

I say, 'I must go to the loo.'

'Yes, of course!' She tells me eagerly: 'Straight at the top of the stairs.'

I close the door of the bathroom my husband frequents, where he must have shaved on those mornings after all the nights he's spent away. He's practically half moved in, she said. I open the cabinet, and sure enough, there are shaving things on its shelves.

I step quietly along the narrow landing past the room with the sleeping child towards the bigger front bedroom. There's the plain double bed where they must lie together, and, sure enough, things of his lying around, clothes belonging to him hanging over a chair . . .

She jumps when I appear in the living-room doorway.

She's been crying, for herself and for me and for the whole ugly mess that we're caught in.

I say, 'I haven't asked you, what do you do?'

She half-laughs. 'Exactly. As if we're only defined by our relationship with him! This is what he's done to us!'

She becomes serious. 'I mean, truly: I do love him, but I *could* live without him, because I don't define myself by him. What I define myself by is my work.'

She adds, 'I'm a counsellor, actually.'

I'm taken aback. I have to say I'm stung. The way she says it, she's implying: *Like you*, and it's an apology, for knowing so much more about me than I know about her.

'Hah. You met him through his work then, like I did.'

She nods. 'Though actually now I'm working with female abuse survivors—up at the Enfield Centre.'

I double-take again. 'I *know* the women who run the Enfield Centre!'

She nods again. 'Yes, I know, I've heard them mention you, but with all the secrecy . . . '

And the look she gives me says: *If it hadn't been for all the secrecy we could have been friends . . . If it hadn't been for the way he divided us . . .*

She says wryly, almost bitterly, 'We have a lot in common, don't we?'

There's silence as we both digest it.

Then: 'So how long has it been going on?'

'Two years.'

For a moment I'm speechless. 'Well, I can't deny then that you do have a claim to him.'

She jumps up, anxious. 'No, no! I keep saying: I'm not making any *claim*! The choice has to be his!'

I contemplate her. 'Well, all I can say is, if it's you he chooses, then good luck to you.'

She's all empathy and sympathy. She's all vindicated sisterhood.

She says, 'And to think that the reason he gave me for not telling you was that you'd take revenge!'

She can't quite see me as I turn on the path, and it's not just the sun in her face, it's the dark glasses I haven't taken off once, merely lifted now and then to poke beneath them and dab at my eyes. She never once saw my eyes. It's the role I came in: he wanted cliché, he could have it—dark-red lips, bitch-painted nails, killer heels. Straight away it unnerved her, and not in the clichéd conventional way: she found it pathetic, and so it put her off guard.

I pan my shades in her direction. She blinks, squints, her blond hair glistening.

I say, 'I don't intend to be a victim, you know.'

'No, of course not!' she cries with grateful relief.

Sun falls on the elderberry clusters, red veins dripping black blood. I move away beneath the tree, through the tangle of black shadows.

She doesn't know that when I found that hair on his jacket I plucked it off, held it aloft, a gold worm hooked and wriggling on a current of air. He watched speechless, admitting nothing, but understanding everything, as I bore it like a sacrifice to the fire and ceremoniously dropped it in. We both stood and listened to it crackle.

I'm watching from my car in the dark late-afternoon as she leaves the Enfield Centre.

It's her he chose, the woman who could live without him, who said she didn't want to claim him. Once the game was up, he moved out altogether and into hers.

She doesn't notice me. She once knew more about me than I knew about her, but she still won't recognise me. She never really saw me that day, the bitch who stole my things and then snatched away my husband, who pulls his lithe pale limbs around her, whose brats he left my bed to go to, trashing his past as a parent with me. Unaware, she gets into her car, the woman who did all this and then thought she could get treated like my sister, pious mealy-mouthed cow.

I want to kill her. I start up quickly and bear down as she slows at the entrance. I see my lights flash like dragon's eyes in her mirror, I see her head jerk up in alarm. As she accelerates I'm right on her tail.

She can't lose me. I keep my foot down, we're doing fifty, she's guessed it's me, but I'm a roaring impersonal dragon behind her, I can feel her terror through all that hot metal.

At last I slow, I won't kill myself too. I let her go for now, the woman who says she'd rather be defined by her work.

I'm watching again the day she's told in no uncertain terms that her services are no longer welcome at the centre. She comes down the steps, her face a white smudge of shock.

I knew it wouldn't play well with my women contacts at the centre. I knew that when I pointed out to them that for two whole years she'd colluded with a man's abuse of another woman, they'd feel that it compromised her position as a counsellor to women abused by men. I knew they'd feel she could no longer be trusted, especially when I drew their attention to the fact that for all that time she'd carefully deceived them too. And as they said then themselves (veterans as they are of the old Sisterhood days): in view of my recent state, and the crucial time that I've consequently lost with my own female clients, she's damaged the cause and hampered a lot of other women's lives . . .

She crosses the car park like a sleepwalker doomed.

He's moving back home.

I knew exactly how she'd feel. I knew she'd consider that ultimately it wasn't I but he who had ruined her career. That if he hadn't behaved in the way that he did, then I'd never have been driven to take revenge.

Sisterhood, eh?

Who's Singing?

Who's that singing?

Not the Professor, the Professor of Medicine, you wouldn't catch him at it, there's no space in his head for it, his head full of thoughts about renal failure and growth retardation. His brow is knotted on a mind he has honed. He has no time for inessentials. He is concerned with life and death matters.

That's Lucy singing. Auxiliary Nurse Lucy up on Women's Medical, the Professor's firm. She's singing bawdy songs while banging round the sluice room; that's not allowed, this is not a place for singing, and if she doesn't watch it she'll be out on her ear. The Professor wouldn't notice, though: he's far too busy, and concerned with more essential things.

The Professor's wife hums a bit: hanging out the washing, hoeing her rows of vegetable seedlings, stopping and starting, the same three bars she'll hum, over and over again, doesn't *sing* exactly. She doesn't know she's humming: her head is full of gossip.

But what about Avril? Avril, whose garden backs onto the Professor's? Now there's a singer for you! A real professional!

[88]

And she doesn't mind you knowing it: if you go to her house (on a formal invitation), she'll show you a disc she has made from the cover of which she smiles resplendent behind a title which proves it conclusively: *Avril Sings*.

You won't hear her singing, though. When Avril sings she sings with purpose and control, on the stage and concert platform, not in city gardens. When she's in the garden all you'll hear is the snapping-off of rose heads, the ones past their best and beginning to go papery (she won't have any truck with them), and the brisk little scrape of her high-heeled fluffy slippers. But if you're not really listening because your head is full of the latest ideas on bone development and calcium deficiency, you'll tend not to hear, and she'll catch you out before you can escape and call you, 'Hello there, Professor!' and want to know if you think there'll be a plague of greenfly, and why do you think the roses are so poor this year, half of them dying before they've even opened, all papery on the outside and squashy in the middle—do you think it's the strange weather?

You suppose that yes, it could be the weather, an icy spring with flurries of snowflakes when you might expect petals, and blossom, when it came, stunted and greyish, a bleak dandruff in corners, and all the vegetation way behind; then suddenly a heat wave, exploding one day and going on ever since, the longest anyone says they've ever known.

Avril makes towards him over the rockery, wobbling in her slippers—nearly falling once or twice—bearing a rosebud like a great pink boil and squeezing it to show him, and when she reaches the fence she says she's glad she's caught him: it's these mouth ulcers she's suffering—he'll understand she needs a healthy mouth in her profession—and she leans across the fence and puts both fingers in her mouth, and pulls her lower lip down, right there in the garden.

The Professor isn't pleased to be demanded of a consultation and a diagnosis and a quick efficient remedy, miles from the consulting room without the aid of examining equipment or the desired professional medical relationship. He comments later to his wife, who is humming at the sink, that a medical man, unless he is constantly on his guard, is prey to much abuse. Anyway, mouth ulcers are not the Professor's thing.

The Professor's interest is Growth and Development, and chemical excesses and elemental deficiencies, and why people live, and why they die. Not mouth ulcers. Also fatness and thinness come into the Professor's subject (a bit).

Avril is fat, or at least pleasantly plump. They say that that is useful in a singer. Avril bakes cakes for her stout family to thrive on, and in August she'll make extra for a garden party to which all the neighbourhood will come (on a formal invitation). She's sure of good weather, of an evening for all to relax and expand in, the weather men say so, and by now everyone's lost the habit of wondering when there'll be rain: all you see looking up are the plane tracks like scabies on the skin of the sky— and some people wonder if, since it's a party, Avril might jut give them all a song.

'Hello there!' Avril calls the Professor, and hopes he can make it in spite of being so busy, and has he heard, we're in for a plague of ladybirds, it seems they thrive on greenfly?

This month the Professor is working late every night, bent at his desk to complete his paper on Post-Pubertal Catch-Up Growth. His wife's getting bored, and she will interrupt him, coming in with gossip. One night she stops in his doorway and says: 'The party's off. It seems that Avril isn't very well.'

Now here's a funny thing. Look at the lawn, in the middle of July, and see it is scattered with little grey scales: leaves have dried up and fallen off, long before their time.

'Hello there, Professor!' It just isn't wise for the Professor to wander with his thoughts in the garden. Avril wonders what on earth these are, all over the plants, scaly and ridged like little black scabs; does he suppose they're the ladybird larvae? And by the way, she expects he'd like to know she went to her own doctor as he suggested, and while she was there he got interested in her other little problem, and the long and the short is she's coming into hospital, and perhaps he can tell her what it will entail, this operation she'll be having?

The Professor's work is diagnosis and deduction, not straight-forward routine surgery. There's a papery look to the skin of Avril's face. It's a telltale sign.

Of course, she's written to tell them she can't go when they want her, she's got rehearsals beginning then; she'll have to go sooner or not at all—well, as the Professor says, it's only a routine thing, and it's all-important that she's there next month to sing.

The Professor tells his wife who is crooning in the kitchen that Avril has extended a formal invitation to his colleague the surgeon to perform on her person a routine procedure far earlier than he ever could have hoped.

The Professor's wife asks him: 'Is she feeling very ill?'

Who's that singing?

It's Lucy, the auxiliary nurse, whose just been moved from Women's Medical—no wonder they got rid of her, listen to her banging round and yelling, Sister will swing for her. And who could possibly sing in the heat of this ward?

You're not to open the windows, Sister's a stickler, dead against petrol fumes, and you'll interfere with the air con and the system will break down. The important patient, the one with all the poshest flowers, the one they say is famous, she's caused a fuss already on that score.

'Excuse me, Sister!' There she sits in all her splendour, in her bright pink lipstick and her fluffy lacy top—who'd have thought she's had an operation? She wants to inform Sister that in her opinion, if the air conditioning can't reduce this heat it may as well break down: see, all her flowers will wilt, her lovely freesias sent this morning from the Chorus; she's beginning to think she may make a complaint or two in some official quarter. She nods her head sharply to indicate that a complaint from her would not go unnoticed.

Well, that won't wash with Sister; in fact that's bound to have done it with Sister, you'll know that if you're Lucy and you've spent the last two days never getting on the right side of Sister. Though it does seem to Lucy that Sister's got a bit to beef about: ever since this morning when the famous opera singer had her post-op bed wash, and sat up in bed, and the flowers started arriving, it's been, 'Excuse me, Nurse!' and could Lucy fetch a vase? And Lucy's been down to the Domestic goodness knows how many times, sweating in her overall, and now and then singing, puffing back to be told to arrange them on the windowsill, or the table, or the cabinet, and feeling a bit put upon.

She's very full of herself, this famous opera singer. People say she jumped the waiting list, through being so important, which doesn't seem right when Lucy's Aunt Eileen had to wait three years, by which time she could hardly walk to the corner shop. That's what Lucy thinks, bashing rose stems on the bottoms of vases, like arrows on bulls-eyes.

Lucy jumps. Who should walk in, but the Professor of Medicine!

Lucy scurries off in case he should recognise her. He nods towards Sister, and then makes straight for the bed of the famous opera singer! Listen to her: 'Hello there!' before he even gets there! Just like old friends! A purely social visit!

Sister, watching from the office, turns away, tight-lipped.

Back home in the city suburb the sky in the evening gets whiter and tighter, and now there's no one lurking, dead-heading the roses when the Professor wanders out before dinner, ordering his thoughts for his talk on Critical Periods for Growth Retardation and Growth Compensation. He goes undisturbed past the peas that came to just nothing, rows of crushed tissue with crinkled white pods. The only sound close at hand is his own feet brushing in the ashy leaves.

At dinner his wife asks: 'Did you go to see Avril?'

He is glad to report that Avril has extended her routine ruthless cosiness into the sphere of abdominal surgery: don't worry, she's thriving on it.

He'll go again then? she ventures, to which he retorts there'll hardly be a chance, she's quite disgustingly fit, she'll be discharged in no time. And anyway, the woman's damned embarrassing.

Some days later in the dusk the Professor's wife stands with her hose trained on her runner beans and peers at Avril's garden, squints across the rose heads like luminous pimples. And peers harder, and drops her arm so the spray is misdirected.

In the house she asks her husband: 'Why is that vine on Avril's porch dying?'

The Professor, who was working, and has been interrupted, replies that vegetables and vines are her thing, not his. Perhaps it needs a water?

But she gave it a water, two days ago when it started to droop. You'd think it would have bucked up then. And isn't it catch-up growth that's just his thing?

The Professor explains, with one eye on his paper, that one question so far unresolved by researchers is whether, post-starvation, a subject will ever achieve its full potential.

'Well, it's hardly doing that. The damn thing is dying.'

In that case, he tells her, she probably missed its Critical Period. She simply didn't water it in time.

The Professor gives up. He's had too much interruption. Besides, he has an early start in the morning, with a lecture on Cell Renewal and Gangrenous Tissue. They lock the doors.

But it's hotter than ever, and the windows upstairs have to be wide open. The Professor's wife can't sleep: out there the darkness seems to be throbbing. A huge bubble of sound erupts away at the airport, and then directly above a plane scalpels the sky. Fine poisonous jet fumes spore across the gardens. Wide-awake with the sheets off, she says, 'Those jet fumes, altering the atmosphere.'

The Professor doesn't answer.

The ground's cracking open. Roots are displaced, and the vines above wither.

In the City Hospital someone needs some air. Lucy, humming very quietly in deference to night duty, passes down the ward and hears the low voice:

'Excuse me, Nurse!'

Trust the famous opera singer to be awake with her pillows up, her face luminous in the dimmed light. After a pause, in which she waits for Lucy to bend very close to her, she says, 'There's just no air in here.'

Well, she's sorry, love, says Lucy, but you know what Sister'll tell you: if you open the windows the fans'll give up altogether, first the ones in here and then, one after the other, all the fans around the hospital, and we'd be worse off than ever, though Lucy can forgive her hardly believing it, why Lucy herself is melting like wax inside her brown overall, and look at those flowers there, every one of them wilting! Perhaps she'd like to sit up a bit more and have a drink of water?

Lucy takes her weight to help prop her up a bit.

Lucy says shortly: 'I'll go and fetch Sister.'

Sister swings down the aisle, bats around the bed end, Lucy scrabbling behind her, and wants to know, what's this then, shouldn't we be asleep by now, it's no good complaining, dear, this heat is something we've all got to suffer—perhaps a little sleeping pill would help?

And then bats off again, standing no nonsense, knowing which patients you've got to be on your guard against.

Lucy stands in the centre aisle. Stock-still.

She's not humming.

Dry leaves peel away and flake across the Professor's roof. His wife goes on to the hump of his body: 'No one foresaw that, did they, busy working away on their scientific inventions? Never entered their heads they might mess up the weather.'

The Professor still doesn't answer. He's fast asleep.

She's dropping off at last when a door slams nearby at the back, voices shout briefly, and a car revs up and roars away.

At breakfast the Professor looks up from his diary to see his wife in the doorway, back from catching the milkman who always brings gossip.

She says to him faintly: 'Avril is dead.'

Dead. That's a scandal. Well, wasn't she quite famous? Yes, look in her notes, a little card with a portrait, pinned to her letter requesting early admission, a famous contralto resplendent and smiling.

How did it happen? How did a healthy (famous) patient, having sailed with ease through a routine operation and then sat smiling like a bright ripe plum, suddenly just die? Overnight, fill up with infection, so that when the emergency officer injected her body, she burst like a pimple?

If you asked Lucy, watching from the store room, remembering her face like a pool of pus in the night, she'd say yes, it's a scandal, and also very sad—think of the poor Professor, wasn't she a friend of his? Oh yes, it's a scandal, but in a funny way there's something makes it not surprising in a famous opera singer who'd never in a million years get up right there and give you all a song.

Not that anyone asks Lucy, she's only an auxiliary, and a bad one at that, who soon won't be here if you wanted to ask her, she's got the sack for being such a bad one, for banging and singing in all the wrong places.

Which means it doesn't matter any more. She sets up singing.

Acknowledgements

'Condensed Metaphysics' was first published in *London Magazine*, 'The Shooting Script' (under a different title and the name Nell Johnson) in *Metropolitan*, 'Daniel Smith Disappears off the Face of the Earth' in *Staple*, 'Power' in *Northern Lights* (Lancaster House) and in *Power* (Honno), and 'Holding Hands' in *Paris Transcontinental*. 'Compass and Torch' was a prizewinner in the London Writers' Inc. competition and appeared on *East of the Web* (www.eastoftheweb.com). 'Star Things' was a prizewinner in the Listowel Writers' Festival short story competition and was published in *Stand* and subsequently in *Best Short Stories from Stand Magazine* (Methuen). 'Leaf Memory' was included in *Firebird 3* (Penguin), and 'A Glossary of Bread' was published on *East of the Web* and in *Stand*, and made the finals of the Moondance International Film Festival short story competition. 'Going Back' appeared in *Bananas* and 'The Way to Behave' in *Bitch Lit* (Crocus). 'Who's Singing?' was a runner-up in a BBC Radio 3 competition and broadcast on Radio 3, and later published in *The Literary Review*.

My thanks go to the editors of the above publications and of other publications in which my stories have appeared. Thanks also to those who have given me support, both moral and practical, in my writing: John Ashbrook, Doris Johnson, Anne Barrick, Matthew White, Ben White, Eileen Simpson, Michael Schmidt, Richard Francis, Debbie Freeman, Alex Barr, Adèle Geras, Julia Segal and Dan Segal. Special thanks to Ailsa Cox for literary companionship and stimulation during our co-editorship of the short-story magazine *Metropolitan*. I am indebted to Jen Hamilton-Emery for doing the magic and making this book happen.